THE NOWHERE THIEF

ALICE M. ROSS

nosy crow

First published in the UK in 2023 by Nosy Crow Ltd
Wheat Wharf, 27a Shad Thames,
London, SE1 2XZ, UK

Nosy Crow Eireann Ltd
44 Orchard Grove, Kenmare,
Co Kerry, V93 FY22, Ireland

ISBN: 978 1 83994 376 8

A CIP catalogue record for this book will be available from the British Library.

Printed and bound in Great Britain by Clays Ltd, Elcograf S.p.A.
Typeset by Tiger Media

Papers used by Nosy Crow are made from wood grown in sustainable forests.

3 5 7 9 10 8 6 4 2

www.nosycrow.com

To my daughter, Greta

Chapter 1

Elsbeth tiptoed through the empty kitchen as quietly as she could. Crayon drawings of stick men with oversized heads were stuck to the fridge. Plastic alphabet letters spelled out *DOG* and *MUMMY*. Some had fallen on the floor and hadn't been tidied up. A smell of burnt marmalade and roasted coffee wafted along the dusty ray of morning light cast through the window. But whoever lived there seemed to be out. Empty houses were starting to feel familiar to Elsbeth.

She pulled open a drawer. Knives and forks glinted like Christmas tree ornaments. Elsbeth seized a handful and stuffed them in her backpack. The metal alloys from other Somewheres were often unusual and could probably be passed off as rare antiques at home.

The last thing she picked up was a small spoon with a cartoon mouse on the handle. She saw her face reflected upside down in it, like an alien. Elsbeth looked at it for a second, then put it back in the drawer. She paused, pulled two adult knives and forks from her backpack and put those back too.

A clock on the counter with a cat's face struck quarter to nine and let out a mechanical miaow. As if on cue, a real cat padded up to Elsbeth and miaowed too. Was it telling her it hadn't been fed? There was something strange about it, though. Elsbeth frowned, staring at it. She realised with a start that it had two tails.

"I should take *you* back with me," she told it, keeping her voice low. The cat flicked both its tails in annoyance.

There was a rumble outside. Something was moving over gravel. Elsbeth ducked, then raised her head to peek out of the window. A mother and a little boy were getting out of a big black car, singing a song. *One, two, buckle your shoe.*

She had to get out of here. Elsbeth had never been caught before and she wasn't about to start now. She zipped her backpack up and turned round. *Three, four, knock at the door.*

Elsbeth heard the child laughing at the front of the house. Too close. But a nagging feeling that she had missed something made her pause and look back at the counter. The cat clock also had two tails. She could definitely sell that at the shop. She grabbed it. The front door slammed and the padding of tiny feet grew nearer. *Five, six, pick up sticks.* Elsbeth moved swiftly back to the opening. But she wasn't fast enough.

A little boy stood in the kitchen doorway, looking quizzical. He had a smear of jam on his nose. It hit Elsbeth that while this place wasn't real to her, it was to him. This was his house. *I left your spoon*, Elsbeth thought. The boy gazed back. *I'm just a twelve-year-old girl*, she wanted to tell him. *I'm not really a thief.*

Holding her breath, she put a finger in front of her lips. He mimicked her, smiling, and she felt relieved.

Heels clicked on the hardwood floor behind him. The boy's mother was coming. Elsbeth edged towards the door and hovered at the opening, which felt like tiny pinpricks all over her skin. Just as the mother walked into the room and gasped, Elsbeth stepped into the shimmer.

And suddenly she was somewhere else entirely. A dark and empty place. This was not a Somewhere, but Nowhere. The air was cold and scentless. When she tried to walk, her legs felt heavier than usual, as if she were moving along the bottom of the seabed. It would have felt a lot scarier in here if it weren't for the silent fireworks show taking place in front of Elsbeth. She was standing in front of a huge sphere, and with every step she took the fireworks rearranged themselves, their colours slightly different. Elsbeth stood outside the sphere, looking in. She'd been in here so much in the past week it almost felt normal. Almost.

She stepped carefully to the left. The colours in front of her shifted. It was like looking at a kaleidoscope. Like the one Mum had given her for her eighth birthday. Mum had said it reminded her of Elsbeth. She knew Mum was talking about her eyes, which changed colour from blue to green to grey depending on what she was wearing. People often commented on it, but it wasn't always a compliment.

So far, Elsbeth hadn't ever walked very far here, in Nowhere. She was too scared of never finding her way home.

She peered at the kaleidoscope. The colours were different depending on where she stood, and she'd worked out that when she found the right mix of colours, she could go forward into her Somewhere – back home. Right now there were two main colours: purple blobs like a bunch of grapes tossed in the air and swirls of green emerald that reminded her of the engagement rings for sale in her shop. They looked like they belonged to her Somewhere but it was hard to tell for sure. She took a tentative step forward, and winced as the opening sucked her through. She realised too late that she was wrong.

Elsbeth stood in another kitchen. In a different Somewhere. But no little boy was going to disturb her here. The place was abandoned. There were empty sockets and stains on the wall where the fridge used to be. The air felt cold and stale. Elsbeth opened a drawer just to check. Empty. The house stood on a hill again – while the Somewhere was different, the geography was the same. But something was wrong. The sea level was much higher up the hill here. Waves lapped at the bottom of the long garden. She heard glass smashing somewhere in the distance, then a scream that made her jump. Mum said you should take long deep breaths to calm down when you felt nervous and Elsbeth did that now. *You can always get away whenever you need to*, she reminded herself.

She backed into the opening, feeling relieved to be back in Nowhere. She stared at the colours. They were still a mix of purple and green, grapes and rings, but she couldn't tell what the right combination was for *her* Somewhere. Maybe there was too much purple? She moved slightly to the left and stepped forward.

She sucked her breath in and tried not to cry out. She was standing in ice-cold water up to her knees. This was definitely not right. The kitchen in this Somewhere was in even worse condition than the last one. And there was an overpowering smell of mould. Elsbeth glanced out of the window and was shocked to see that the sea had risen as if it were swallowing the land. Little waves were licking round chimneys of houses lower down the hill that had been above ground in the last Somewhere. The garden, if there was one, was completely covered in water. A small black fish swam past her foot. Just beyond it, a picture frame bobbed up and down in the water. A picture of a boy with glasses and no front teeth grinned up at her. Her acquisitive instinct kicked in and she waded closer to look at it properly. But the frame was wooden and had probably been in the water far too long to be worth anything. She was wasting time.

Then she felt an odd sucking feeling round her legs. She looked down. The water in the kitchen was getting shallower, as if she were in a bath and someone had pulled the plug. Elsbeth turned round, and gasped. A wave like a wall was surging across the rooftops below, gathering strength as it headed straight for the kitchen. Elsbeth stumbled towards the opening. The thick water and the heavy backpack were slowing her down. She had a moment of panic. What if she *couldn't* always get away? The wave crashed into the glass windows of the kitchen and the water hit her waist with a sharp slap as she threw herself into Nowhere.

It felt just like someone had flicked a switch. The wave was gone, and Elsbeth felt her heart shake her body in the dark silence. That had been close. She shuddered. Too close. She needed to get home. Elsbeth took deep breaths to calm herself down and tried to think. Perhaps she had been going the wrong way. She'd been taking steps to the left, but maybe her Somewhere was back towards the right. She took three large steps the other way and peered back at the kaleidoscope. Third time lucky. She stepped forward.

The dry floor was the first thing she noticed. That was a good sign. Elsbeth looked around the room. This kitchen looked familiar.

She glanced at the wooden table. She had to check. Somewheres close to each other could be so similar. Even people sometimes looked alike – like versions of each other. But, sure enough, the mark she'd carved with her penknife earlier was still there. It had been sunny when she left, and now dark storm clouds were moving in, but she was finally back home. That had been the closest that Elsbeth had come to getting lost in Nowhere. And it was because she'd gone too far, she realised. She had to be more careful. Take smaller steps. Focus more on the colours in the kaleidoscope. They swirled about so much it was difficult to tell them apart, but she was sure that each Somewhere had its own distinctive pattern. She would get to recognise hers soon enough, she was sure of it.

Elsbeth made another rule for herself. *No more places with kids*. She didn't like the way she'd felt when that toddler had looked at her.

She readjusted the heavy backpack, pulling the straps tighter, and looked around the room. On the wall hung a painting with lots of red lines and blue dots that looked like a child had made it. Elsbeth suspected it was very expensive. A haughty-looking brass horse and a statuette of a naked woman sat on the table. She could definitely sell those at the shop. But Elsbeth knew better than to take anything from her own Somewhere, even if it was from an empty house.

The occupants of this house, whoever they were, had left the door unlocked, making it easy for Elsbeth to get in. Second homers, Mum called them. They loved to tell their Lunden friends how welcoming the seaside villagers were. Such a sense of community, such a safe neighbourhood. The tourist homes had the best views of the sea, and most people only came to stay in them for the summer. Mum said it was ridiculous and that the town should set them aside for residents. But the real residents couldn't afford to live in houses this nice.

Suddenly Elsbeth felt a prickle at the back of her neck. She whipped round. The opening shimmered behind her like a thousand tiny diamonds sewn on to the air. For a second she thought she glimpsed a dark figure, standing motionless. Was it just her, or was the figure holding out its hand to her? But of course it couldn't be. *Don't be so stupid*, she told herself. As she looked at it, the figure faded away and the opening sealed up like a pool of water righting itself after a stone was thrown in. It must have been her reflection. But it left her feeling odd, as if an insect was between her shoulder blades.

The church bells on top of the hill began to bong. Seven, eight, nine. She was later than she thought. Elsbeth dashed out of the unlocked back door and into the dark, thickening storm outside.

◆

Elsbeth slammed the shop door against the howling sea air at her back. The silence was sudden. She was drenched, though the rain had been warm, and she squinted for a minute as she caught her breath. Then the room she knew as well as Mum's wide smile revealed itself. Most of the lights had been switched on, casting an amber glow. Copper plates with old engravings shone down from the walls, and teak furniture soaked up what little daylight fought its way through the shutters. Silver candlesticks, opal necklaces and gilded picture frames cluttered every surface. It was like a hundred families had piled their living rooms together, with everything overlapping. It was probably what all the Somewheres would look like, if you could see them all at once. Customers were sometimes a little overwhelmed by the amount of stuff, but Elsbeth knew where everything was like the back of her hand.

The incense stick that Elsbeth's mum lit every morning was already filling the shop with its musky smell. In the middle of the room at the counter sat Mum, doing her crossword, wrapped in a thick woolly jumper even though it was August.

"Sorry I'm late," Elsbeth panted. She slung the backpack off and it clunked on to the floor. It was the summer holidays and she'd promised to help Mum in the shop in the mornings. It was supposed to be tourist season, and they were supposed to be busier than usual. So far, Elsbeth hadn't seen much sign of it.

Mum sighed. "Don't worry, darling. It seems quiet today. Again."

Last summer, tourists had pottered into the shop first thing, on their way to or from breakfast. This year, the mornings had been deadly quiet.

The shop windows rattled suddenly, as if tiny pebbles were being thrown at them. "And a freak summer hailstorm is all we need to scare the tourists off," Mum added. A hairpin was already making its way out of Mum's hair towards the countertop. It was remarkable, thought Elsbeth, how early in the day the hairpins seemed to want to escape.

Mum tugged at her hair and the hairpin took advantage of the moment to break free, tinkling down to the floor. She read aloud from her crossword. "*Star sign commonly associated with a goat. Nine letters.*"

"Capricorn," said Elsbeth. She looked at Mum. Her hair seemed greyer. Mum used to always say her hair was mouse brown like Elsbeth's. But that had never made any sense. All the mice Elsbeth had ever seen were grey. Now Mum joked that she really did have mouse hair.

"Maybe we should do a summer sale. Get rid of some of the stuff that's been here for years." Mum laughed, but it wasn't a real laugh.

Elsbeth looked at the eighteenth-century sideboard that Mum said she held on to when she took her first steps. She could trace every scratch on the wood with her eyes shut. If someone ever actually wanted to buy it, Mum would be horrified. Most of the antiques had been there for years. Turnover in their sleepy shop wasn't particularly high. In the winter months, when tourists stayed away, a whole day could go past without a single customer.

But this week it looked a little different. Elsbeth could see new things she'd brought back from other Somewheres. There was the oval picture frame with metal brambles woven round the edges that she'd swiped from an empty house yesterday. The metal was unusually soft. So soft that Elsbeth had been able to push the brambles away from the frame to make it look less messy. Looking at it again, she could have sworn the brambles had moved back a bit, like tentacles wrapping round a creature. Next to the frame sat a rock she'd found smashed open on a beach in another Somewhere. The light caught the green stones inside it, little stalagmites pulsating with their own quiet energy.

Behind that was the art deco dressing table with metal peacocks emerging either side of the mirror where she used to play dressing-up and pretend to be a pirate. Faded light from the street hit the mirror and Elsbeth saw herself looking gloomy in it. Her straggly curls were coming loose from her ponytail – she was determined not to go down the hairpin route. Even so, for a second she could see Mum's face in hers. But she thought she looked more like her dad, who had died before she was born. The only picture that Mum had of him stood on the dressing table: Mum, barely out of her teens, and Dad, squinting into the sun, on holiday in Greece, a white archway behind them. The peacocks stared at her dispassionately. She never wanted anyone to buy them either.

"I'll work harder, I promise," she told Mum, trying to sound confident.

"Oh, Elsbeth. You're working hard enough already. But we can practise again today. When the next customer comes in, you can do the selling. You know as much about everything in here as I do. Perhaps more."

Elsbeth sighed. Mum said she should be more confident with customers. But Elsbeth hated selling things. It felt so fake. Still, it had to be done; she knew that.

As if on cue, there was a tinkle at the front door. They both looked round hopefully. But it wasn't a customer.

In strode Mr Lennox, the landlord who owned half the high street. He had to lower his head to get through the doorway, then shook the water off it roughly, like a dog.

"Ah, Mrs Tawney. You're finally in. You've been rather hard to get hold of," he barked. The dainty sherry glasses in the glass cabinet shivered as he spoke.

Mum raised an eyebrow. "We are always here during opening hours, Mr Lennox. And I don't appreciate the suggestion I might be hiding from you."

"I might hide from myself too, if I owed me as much money as you do," Mr Lennox said. He was very tall and always stood with his feet a little too far apart, as if he were about to burst into song. The shop seemed a lot smaller with him in it. The belt he was wearing was fake leather, Elsbeth noted with a critical eye. She wondered what the point was of having so much money and wearing a belt that she could have picked up at a car boot sale for less than a crown.

"You'll know why I'm here, Mrs Tawney," Mr Lennox continued. He tapped his wrist exaggeratedly. "Rent for August is due. *Overdue*, as I'm sure you are aware."

For a man so rich he was remarkably attentive to small bills like theirs, Elsbeth thought. Perhaps that was why he was rich.

"As I said to you on the phone, Mr Lennox, I just need a little more time," said Mum. "The tourist season has been slow, and your constant rent increases for no apparent reason are not helping."

Mr Lennox cut Mum off. "I just passed Giselle's Glassware on the way here. That new place, selling the fancy handmade vases and whatnot. Bustling with the Lunden crowd, it was. Didn't seem slow at all. No, I'm not buying that, Mrs Tawney." He looked around the shop critically, and Elsbeth saw for the first time that there was a faint layer of dust over most of the items. "The problem is this shop, not the customers. Same old dull inventory. Why, I'm not sure there's been anything new in here for years!"

Elsbeth moved a little to position herself in front of the bramble picture frame. She didn't want Mum's attention drawn to it right now.

Mum paused, then said, "I will have the rent for you by the end of the week, Mr Lennox."

"And how do you propose to do that then?"

"How I get the money, Mr Lennox, is none of your business. Suffice to say you will have it. Now, I suggest you leave us in peace so that we might get on with our business."

Mr Lennox made a sort of *pfft* sound that suggested

what his feelings were about that, and walked away. As if he couldn't resist, though, he turned back at the door and added, "The law is on my side, Mrs Tawney. If I don't get that money, I'll serve you with an eviction notice."

Mr Lennox slammed the door as he left and Elsbeth looked at Mum. Her lips were pursed, and she was staring at a point on the floor somewhere behind Elsbeth.

"Mum?"

"Can you mind the shop for a little while, darling? I'm going to go through some bits and bobs in the attic and see what I can do."

"Bits and bobs?"

"Savings," said Mum vaguely. "We have some old policies here and there. I just need to find the details." She headed towards the stairs at the back of the shop.

"Mum," Elsbeth said, more firmly this time.

Mum turned round. "Don't worry, darling. I'm going to sort this out. That Mr Lennox is an old bully. He's not evicting us. He's all talk and bluster. OK?"

Elsbeth gave Mum a smile, because she felt she expected her to. "OK."

Mum went upstairs, and Elsbeth's smile faded. Neither of them had been saying how they really felt.

They'd just been trying to make each other feel better. Mr Lennox's words hung in her head. The high street had been full of tourists, he'd said. So why weren't they coming into their shop? Her eye fell on the green rock she had picked up in the Somewhere by the beach. If the tourists knew they had things like this in here, they'd flock in, she was sure of it. Elsbeth just had to work out how to let them know.

Chapter 2

It was quiet in the shop. Too quiet. Elsbeth busied herself laying out for display the knives and forks she'd taken from the little boy's Somewhere. But the cat clock with two tails had stopped ticking. She wondered if clocks from other Somewheres didn't work here.

She suddenly remembered that the same thing had happened with the compass Victoria had lent her.

Victoria's Somewhere was where it had all begun. It started by accident, really. It was a couple of years ago now. Elsbeth had been up in the attic with a book, feeling that unusual stillness that came over her whenever she was reading something gripping. And then, all of a sudden, she felt a rush of energy.

She had stood up in surprise. The air around her

seemed to be shimmering, as if she were looking through frosted glass. She took a step forward into the shimmer, and found herself in the kaleidoscope. She didn't know what it was, of course. She still didn't. But she saw the coloured lights and ran towards them, crying out for help.

And a little girl had answered.

Elsbeth realised that she'd escaped from the dark, scary place that she later called Nowhere. The room she was in looked so familiar that at first she thought she was back in her own attic.

Victoria had been in the middle of building a huge tower. She didn't seem scared that Elsbeth had just appeared out of nowhere to play with her. In fact, she was curious. Once they worked out that Elsbeth could get in and out by waiting for the rush of energy at the same spot, they played together a lot. It was easier to play with Victoria than the girls at school. Those girls were already interested in make-up and boys, and didn't have to work in their parents' shops at the weekend. They didn't know or care what art deco was. Even Josie, who used to be Elsbeth's closest friend in the village, said she should use products on her curls to stop them looking so frizzy, and stop wearing baggy clothes that looked like her mum had picked them out.

Mum *had* picked them out, and Elsbeth had not, until then, realised there was anything wrong with that. She had felt the shame of not being in on something all the other girls seemed to intuitively understand.

Victoria was different. Girls in Victoria's Somewhere weren't very into fashion. They were more worried about rising sea levels. Victoria went on weekend camping trips to learn about survival skills. Mascara wasn't a big feature of those trips, as far as Elsbeth could tell. Victoria had a compass she used to take on those camping trips, and she had lent it to Elsbeth as an experiment. They wanted to see if north and south were in the same place in Elsbeth's Somewhere as Victoria's, given that they looked so similar. But as soon as Elsbeth took it back to her attic, it stopped working. And it didn't work when she took it back to Victoria either. She'd felt bad about that.

Victoria couldn't travel the way Elsbeth could. She had tried to follow Elsbeth into the shimmer but it never worked. Even back then, Elsbeth could feel that there was more out there, in Nowhere. But it felt too vast and threatening. To take a short step to Victoria's felt like adventure enough.

Elsbeth wished she could go and see Victoria now and discuss all this with her. But she had promised

Mum to mind the shop. She sighed.

The morning passed slowly. One custo
and bought one of the slag-glass lamps. But Elsbeth was annoyed to see that Mum hadn't updated the price tag on it as they'd discussed. It went for two crowns less than it should have, but she knew you had to sell something at the price stated on the label. Those were the rules. Another customer came in asking if she could pawn her necklace for money, and Elsbeth had to explain, not for the first time, that an antiques shop was not a pawn shop. The woman took this personally and left in a huff.

Occasionally Elsbeth heard Mum crashing about in the attic upstairs and, for a while, in Elsbeth's bedroom. Mum had shoved a load of papers and things that didn't fit in the attic into the chest of drawers in Elsbeth's room, leaving Elsbeth hardly any room for clothes. It also meant that Mum seemed to think Elsbeth's room was half hers, which Elsbeth didn't think was fair.

Finally Elsbeth heard Mum making kitchen sounds next door. She turned the shop sign to CLOSED and went into the back room.

It was pasties, stuffed with potatoes and cheese, for lunch. Mum made a batch of them every week – it was her signature dish. Mum sat at the table with a cup of tea, pen in hand. "*Border edifice built in Roman times. Eight, four,*" she said without looking up.

"Hadrian's Wall," Elsbeth said. She was sure Mum knew that one herself. Sometimes she asked stuff just to test her. It was like living with a teacher.

She sat down, and Mum jumped up and went to put the kettle on at the stove. The match snapped as she struck it. The next one did too. "Drat!" she snapped, putting her hands on the counter and closing her eyes. The hairpins were sticking out higgledy-piggledy, as if someone had scribbled around her head.

"I have to go to Lunden," she announced.

Elsbeth was surprised. Mum hated going to Lunden – she couldn't remember the last time her mum had even left Lewesby. Her family had disapproved of Elsbeth's father and had cut Mum off when she got pregnant. Then Dad had died and Mum had landed in this sleepy village. Now they had nobody but each other. "When?"

"Now," said Mum. "But I should be back in time for dinner."

Elsbeth frowned. "Did you find the savings policies?"

"Yes, but it's complicated. There are penalties for taking the money out early, it seems. I think it best if I go and speak to the bank about it. Perhaps we can come to some arrangement."

Elsbeth looked down at her pasty, still untouched. "Why is the shop struggling so much, Mum?"

Mum sighed. "It's these new shops selling quirky modern things. Everything in here is old. Antiques just aren't that trendy right now, I suppose. And Mr Lennox has put the rent up twice this year already. But we'll cope, darling."

Her mum kissed Elsbeth on the forehead – Elsbeth didn't have her normal urge to pull back – and then grabbed her handbag. "You don't mind looking after the shop this afternoon, do you? The sun's out again after that storm – hopefully that means tourists in the streets. Be brave if the customers ask you anything. Remember, you know more than they do," she said, her hand on the door. She looked at Elsbeth a second longer, then she was gone.

Elsbeth chewed a bite of her pasty thoughtfully. Hopefully it would all be fine. Mum would get their savings out and Mr Lennox would get paid. At least they had savings. But even if Mum got the rent this time, there'd still be next month, and the month after that. Elsbeth sighed, thinking about how quiet the morning had been. The tourists liked new, modern stuff, Mum had said. The things Elsbeth could get from the other Somewheres were certainly unusual. The question was how she was going to get customers into the shop to see them. She no longer had the appetite for her lunch, and went back to the shop, turning the sign to OPEN.

A couple of tourists walked past outside, chattering. They barely gave the shop a glance. Elsbeth wanted to fling the door open and call to them to come in. But she wasn't brave enough. The time ticked by and not a soul came in. To stop a sense of rising panic, Elsbeth thought about something Mum had told her earlier that year. Elsbeth had been upset about not being invited to a sleepover that the girls in her class were having. *Focus on the things you can control, rather than the things you can't,* Mum had said. Then they'd made shortbread together and watched old films all evening instead. And Elsbeth felt it was probably more fun than going to the sleepover anyway.

She looked around the shop, trying to see it critically. How could she make it better? She loved everything being all jumbled up together. It gave her a feeling of exploration. You never knew what you might find: an elephant mug nestling next to a silver butter dish, for example, or a set of mismatched woven rugs rolled up and stacked in a Chinese urn like umbrellas. Some of the smaller items like jewellery were stashed in the cabinets because they'd run out of space to display them, and Elsbeth liked the idea that an enterprising customer might open a drawer and find something they loved. That had never happened, though, come to think of it. She brushed her finger over a decanter and sighed. She'd give the place a good dust.

For the rest of the afternoon Elsbeth busied herself with dusting, which was about as boring as she had expected. No wonder Mum didn't bother. She felt a bit better once she was finished, though. The antiques had an air of expectation, she thought, now that they were clean and sparkling. She owed it to them to find people to buy them.

◆

She was in the back, putting the cleaning supplies away, when the shop bell finally tinkled, just before closing time. "Just a minute!" she called, coming back in. She saw a man inspecting something by the window, his back to her. Then he turned round.

The first thing Elsbeth saw was the moustache. It was long and grey, and twirled up at either end. It was attached to a stern-looking person wearing a hat and a dark-green raincoat that looked like it was made from rubber – certainly not right for a summer's day.

Elsbeth cleared her throat. "Can … can I help you?"

The man looked her up and down and raised an eyebrow. "*You* are an antiques specialist?" His moustache moved when he spoke, as if it had its own opinion about her too.

Elsbeth held her chin up and remembered what Mum had said. *You know more than they do.* She tried a technique she often used: she imagined she had a mask on that disguised her as an adult, giving her just as much right to talk to customers as anyone else. That made her less likely to go red.

The man picked up a long brass object that a normal person might have guessed was a dagger holder. He held it up in front of Elsbeth and asked in a testing sort of way, "Perhaps you can tell me about this piece?"

He had an odd way of leaving long pauses in the middle of his sentences, as if he didn't really believe what he was saying.

"That's one of our best pieces," Elsbeth said promptly. "A brass letter opener from the art nouveau period. Around 1910, we believe, originally from Birmingham."

"Indeed?" The man pulled one side of his moustache out until it was straight, then let it go. Elsbeth half expected to hear a *pop!* as the curl sprang back into place. It was the sort of thing her own messy curls would never do.

"In that case perhaps you can enlighten me as to the origin of this piece here?" The man moved over to the side table where the bramble picture frame stood.

"Victorian. It originally had gold gilt on the frame but that's worn off, as you can see. We're offering it at a very good price."

"Are you now?" the man said, looking directly at Elsbeth. She began to feel a little uncomfortable. She was well aware that both the pieces he had chosen were things she had picked up in the Somewheres – so not art nouveau or Victorian at all. But if she couldn't see the difference, she doubted anyone else could. At least, not the sort of person that normally came into their shop. Her heart sank when he moved to the third piece: the knives and forks she had neatly stacked that morning.

"What can you tell me about these?" The man ran his finger down the sharp edge of one of the knives and Elsbeth winced.

"I bought them at a local auction. They're mid-century modern. From Denmark." Elsbeth instantly regretted being so creative. She hadn't had time to examine them properly and make up something plausible. Instinct made her move in front of the rock with the pulsating green stones so he couldn't see it.

"Presumably you will charge a hefty mark-up?" The man smiled for the first time, but it was not a pleasant experience.

"This is a business, sir."

He looked at her for a moment longer then said, somewhat to Elsbeth's surprise, "I will take them all."

Elsbeth went over to the till and rang up the sale, studying the man as she did so. He held himself very upright and was carrying a travel bag of some sort – he certainly wasn't local but didn't look like a tourist either. His shoes were bright and shiny but she noticed his fingernails were chewed. She chewed her fingernails too, but she was twelve. On a grown-up it seemed odd.

"That's an interesting bird." The man was looking over her shoulder at the shelf behind the till where Mum kept trinkets and a stuffed parrot with bright-blue feathers and a yellow head, like the sun overlooking the sea.

"That's not for sale," said Elsbeth. Then she remembered Mum had said she should make small talk with customers. "Come to get some sea air, have you?" she asked in her best Mum voice.

"Something like that." He didn't seem very interested in small talk. "Do you get new items in often?"

"Quite often," Elsbeth lied.

"If you do get anything … *similar* … to these three items, I'd be very interested. I'll leave you my card. I'm staying at the Seaview Tavern." He said this without looking at Elsbeth.

The shop door tinkled as he left and Elsbeth peered down at the card. NORBERT PERSIMMON it said in a small black font, followed only by a phone number. Elsbeth turned it over. The other side was green, with what looked like a chain necklace printed on it.

The items that Norbert Persimmon had bought were all decades apart – at least, according to what Elsbeth had told him. They had nothing in common at all. Except one thing.

Elsbeth looked at the card again. She had a nasty feeling she knew what he meant by *similar*.

Chapter 3

Elsbeth woke with a start. Bright moonlight shone on to her pillow. A full moon. She never shut her curtains – she liked being woken by the morning light, and there was something extra special about being woken by moonlight. There was a bear in the moon if you looked at it the right way, Mum always said. It was sitting hunched, as if it were eating a pot of honey.

Her kaleidoscope sat on the windowsill, sparkling in the cold, bright light. She remembered Mum giving it to her. "This has always been my treasure," Mum had said. "And now you are my treasure. I think the two of you should be together." Elsbeth had slept clutching it at night for a while after that, before she got older and realised she might break it.

Then it all came back to her. Mum had been stressed when she got home for dinner. The bank hadn't given her any money. Mr Lennox was breathing down their necks. Would they get kicked out of their shop, out of their home? Where would she and Mum go then? Not to Mum's family, that was for sure. She hadn't spoken to them for years. Go to Lunden, make a fresh start? Something secret in Elsbeth yearned for this. To be in a big city, with so much to explore, where she didn't already know everyone and everyone didn't know her. But it would kill Mum to leave here. She knew that. Mum felt safe in Lewesby, and it was their home.

And then there was that strange man, Norbert Persimmon. Elsbeth hadn't told Mum about him at dinner – some sort of instinct had held her back. But now, at that strange time of night when her thoughts felt uncontrollable, she started to worry. He couldn't possibly have known that all those things he bought were from the Somewheres, could he? Perhaps he was an antiques dealer himself, and simply recognised that they were different. But in that case he would have known she was lying about where they were from, so wouldn't he have confronted her, rather than buying them? It didn't make sense.

Still, whoever he was, he was willing to buy things from their shop – unlike basically every other tourist in town. Norbert Persimmon meant more money for her and Mum – he was her chance to help Mum with the rent. So if he wanted more *unusual* stuff, she was going to have to get it for him. As fast as possible. And, she thought, as her eyes closed and she felt herself drifting off to sleep, she knew just the place.

◆

Elsbeth pulled her flannel shirt tighter round her as she walked out on to the high street the next morning. It was still early, before nine, and the sun hadn't yet heated up the day, even though it was August. She had dashed past Mum at breakfast, only stopping to grab a fresh cinnamon bun that Mum had warmed in the oven. Steam rose from the bun in the cold morning air as she wolfed it down hungrily. At the café next door, two locals sat outside despite the chill, eating brunost cheese on rye bread – the local speciality.

The cobbled streets were perfect in their imperfection: tourists from Amerika were always comparing it to Disneyland. She walked under a row of copper signs sticking out into the street like gargoyles, proclaiming the nature of their shop's business. MRS CRADDOCK'S OLD TEACAKES, HANSEN'S BARBERS, VITO'S TAILOR AND

Repair Shop. Elsbeth and Mum knew everyone along the street. Mum was the newcomer, really, arriving just before Elsbeth was born. Many of the other shop families had been there for centuries.

But one family had recently sold up and left. Elsbeth found herself standing outside the empty shopfront. Gry and Adam Osmond had lived here. Gry was beautiful, with black hair in a thousand tiny braids that waved perfectly down to her back. Adam was as pale as a piece of paper and looked like he needed feeding. He had come down from Lunden one weekend as a tourist and had fallen in love with Gry, so the story went, and never looked back. Except one day he did. When Gry got pregnant, Adam said there wasn't enough money in a tourist shop, and they moved together to Lunden, where he had a high-powered job in finance.

Nobody had taken up the new lease yet. Elsbeth peered through the window and saw a few old pieces of cloth and a pincushion like a hedgehog, remnants of the lace-making business Gry's family had been in for centuries. She wondered how much money Mr Lennox was losing having this place empty, and felt a wicked thrill.

Then she went down the passageway at the side of the shop and pushed at the door. It opened.

The idea Elsbeth had had as she lay awake in the night was that if she went to a Somewhere very close by, this would still be a shop – and hopefully not an empty one. She had been thinking about the little boy with the strawberry jam and the cat with two tails. Being in a shop was better than being in someone's house. It felt less personal somehow. And yet even as she thought this Elsbeth knew it wasn't quite right. Her shop felt personal enough to her. But sometimes being in the Somewheres felt like being a different person. A version of Elsbeth who could do or say anything. Something about that scared her.

Elsbeth moved around the dusty room until she felt an opening. She checked her watch. It was eight forty. She wasn't quite sure how time worked in the other Somewheres, but she assumed it was the same. At least, it was always the same time in Victoria's Somewhere. Hopefully that meant it would be too early for there to be any customers in another shop, if there was one, and she could get in and out quickly.

She closed her eyes and felt the familiar hum in the air as the opening materialised. Then she stepped through into Nowhere.

The purple blobs and green swirls of the kaleidoscope flashed in front of her. *Don't go too far*, she reminded herself. She took one small careful step to the right. The colours barely changed as she stepped forward – maybe a smidgen more green – and she wondered if she'd just come out in the empty shop again. It was so hard to know how far to go before the Somewhere was different.

But she felt a surge of achievement as soon as she stepped out. Sure enough, she was in a shop, and it was full of things. And, importantly, no people. It almost looked like an antiques shop, Elsbeth thought. The shelves were filled with little sculptures. She had the funny idea that she might bump into herself in this Somewhere, or Mum, pottering about in another version of their shop.

Of course, this wasn't in the same place as their shop – it was further up the high street. And Elsbeth could see on closer inspection that it wasn't really an antiques shop. The sculptures all looked identical and had clearly been mass-produced. Elsbeth peered at a row of little golden men sitting with their legs crossed and a sort of turban on their heads. One of these would do nicely, she decided. She reached out for one and picked it up.

And all the little golden men's heads swivelled towards her.

Elsbeth dropped the golden man as if it had burned

her. It clanged to the ground and lay on its back, staring at the ceiling. She blinked and looked back at the row of sculptures. They were all staring straight ahead again. Had she just imagined what happened? She reached for the golden man on the ground, though her hand was trembling. Almost immediately a voice bellowed from behind her. "Oh no you *don't*!"

She swung round in horror. A skinny man with a straggly beard dressed in a silver suit stood there, breathing heavily. Elsbeth turned to run. But the man grabbed her arm.

"I don't believe in violence; I really don't," he said as his fingers made dents in her flesh. "But breaking and entering is a serious crime, young lady. I'm going to have to call the Polit."

Elsbeth squirmed in his surprisingly strong grip. Whatever the Polit were, she didn't think she wanted to meet them.

The man half dragged her over to the front of the shop. Elsbeth saw a cobbled street out of the window that looked like her own high street. But instead of shop signs there were security cameras, swivelling around like eyes on the ends of long stalks. The people below them were dressed in drab metallic suits and hurried by, keeping their heads down as if it were raining, though the sun shone brightly. The man twisted Elsbeth's hand and forced her thumb on to a metal plate on the wall next to the door, like a doll he was manoeuvring into place. "There. They've got you now," he said.

But the plate let out a loud honking sound. The man peered closer at it, keeping his grip round Elsbeth's wrist. UNKNOWN flashed the plate, in large red letters.

"That's odd," said the man. He pushed Elsbeth's thumb roughly on to the plate again. UNKNOWN the plate continued to flash.

Suddenly the honking got ten times as loud, as if an alarm had been triggered. The man put his hands to his ears then realised his mistake and grabbed for Elsbeth again. She darted one way then the other but couldn't get to the opening to escape.

Then from behind her came a piercing whistle.

"Over here!"

Both Elsbeth and the man swung round to see a boy with a mane of black hair race through the room and grab the sculpture. Where had he come from?

"Hey! Put that down!" the man shouted.

But the boy was too quick. He grabbed Elsbeth by the wrist. "Come on, let's get out of here!" he shouted. His charcoal eyes flashed at her. Elsbeth didn't have time to think and ran after him. He was heading towards the back of the shop, where the opening was still shimmering gently. The man ran after them but the boy pushed over a chair and the man fell down, howling in anger and clutching his knee.

"You go in first," the boy panted, as he thrust Elsbeth in front of him. "And take this." He pushed the sculpture into her hands and glanced behind him. The man was already up, hopping towards them. "Quickly!"

Elsbeth hugged the sculpture close to her chest and almost fell into the opening, hearing the boy's heavy breathing behind her.

The darkness came. For a second she was aware of a presence nearby, but then it was gone. Had the boy followed her into Nowhere? It was so dark it was hard to see. She patted her free hand on the air around her as if she were performing a mime. But there was nothing solid. The heaviness in Nowhere seemed to silence sound, so she had no idea if the boy was near her or not.

"Hello?" Her voice came out muffled, as if she were under water. She doubted the boy would be able to hear it, even if he were in Nowhere with her. Then Elsbeth felt a sinking feeling. She looked down with a jolt. Had she been standing still too long? She bent down to feel the floor. It felt odd – not particularly solid, a little like standing in soft sand on a beach. She drew her hand back quickly. She didn't want to think about whether it was possible to fall through the floor in Nowhere.

There was nothing to do but go back home. At least this time it was easier. She took a careful step to the left, exactly the same-sized step that she'd taken on the way there, and came out in Gry and Adam's abandoned shop again. That was a relief. She *could* control where she was going if she just paid attention. Her arrival seemed to cause all the dust in the shop to rise into the air, and as it settled Elsbeth saw through the haze that the people outside were dressed in normal clothes, the reassuring street signs back in their places. She thought of the cameras on stalks and shuddered. What had been wrong with that Somewhere? She found she was twisting the sculpture round and round in her hands. It seemed totally inanimate, and she wondered if she had had what Mum sometimes called a "funny turn".

Then she thought about the boy. He had *followed* her. He had *known* about the opening. Was he like her? Or had he just seen her come out and wanted to see how it worked? If that was the case, was he lost somewhere else now? Elsbeth didn't even know how the openings worked for normal people. For her it was like looking into a pool of water and seeing seashells just below the surface. She could feel that they were there, waiting for her to bring them to the surface and open them. But once she did that, did it mean that just anyone could slip through into the kaleidoscope, even if they weren't like her? Victoria hadn't been able to. But maybe other people could. Elsbeth felt a stab of responsibility. Should she have tried to find this boy? But she had already lost track of him in that brief time in Nowhere. He could be anywhere by now.

There were too many thoughts racing around her head. She looked at the sculpture. Its heaviness reassured her. At least she had this. And there was no time to waste. She was going straight to see Norbert Persimmon.

Chapter 4

Elsbeth stepped into the street and was nearly blown back into the empty shop. It had been calm and sunny when she left, but now a strong wind was hurling through the high street. It knocked a woman's hat off and she went scuttling up the street trying to catch it. Elsbeth put her head down into the wind and trudged slowly, as if she were going through heavy snow. This summer storm wasn't as warm as the one yesterday – the wind was biting, and Elsbeth felt tears stream down her cheeks.

By the time she turned off the cobbled high street her hair was sticking out of her head in all directions. She walked into a courtyard and the wind stopped as suddenly as if someone had switched off the radio. Her ears rang from the silence. She was standing in front of a hotel overshadowed by a large wisteria. The Seaview Tavern was improbably named, as every tourist who came to stay there realised immediately. A couple walked out as Elsbeth approached, carrying a map of the town and looking rather dejected.

"Can you tell us the best way to the beach?" the man asked.

"It's about half a mile that way," said Elsbeth, gesturing. The woman looked at the man icily and his shoulders slumped.

Elsbeth walked through the hotel entrance and found herself in a room heavy with dark wooden beams. It seemed appropriate that Mr Persimmon was staying here. She couldn't imagine he had been too bothered about the location. The boy who'd helped her escape was in her head – the flash of charcoal eyes, the mane of black hair – but she couldn't think about that now.

"Yes?" The receptionist stared at Elsbeth. She was a girl herself, really – Elsbeth remembered her from the sixth form last year. Everyone talked about leaving Lewesby and going to Lunden to have adventures when they left school, but clearly not everyone managed it. This girl had been in the popular crowd and Elsbeth remembered envying her – always standing surrounded by friends, laughing at jokes. The girl stared at her blankly. Clearly Elsbeth had not made an impression on her.

Elsbeth tried to smooth her crazed hair down so that she looked more normal. "I … I'm looking for a Mr Persimmon…" She faltered, willing her cheeks not to turn red.

"In the dining hall," the girl said with a bored wave of her hand to the right. Elsbeth went down a corridor into what looked more like an old sitting room, with mismatched chairs and round wooden tables that had tea stains on them. In one corner sat Mr Persimmon. He was wearing slippers and a green padded dressing gown that didn't look too dissimilar to his raincoat. Another guest sat a couple of tables away, fully dressed and giving his breakfast companion a wary look. Mr Persimmon obviously hadn't noticed him at all. He was picking listlessly at some grey, watery eggs and burnt toast. When he looked up and saw Elsbeth, he brightened visibly.

"I hope you haven't ordered coffee," he said. "I don't advise it. Please, sit down."

Elsbeth set the sculpture on the table with a clunk. Her shoulder ached from carrying it. Mr Persimmon looked at it, then up at her.

"It's for sale," she said, feeling awkward and sitting down heavily opposite Mr Persimmon.

"Indeed." Mr Persimmon absently twirled his moustache again and picked up the sculpture. He took a much closer look this time than he had at the things he'd bought yesterday, Elsbeth noticed, making various "hums" and snorts of interest like a pig snuffling for truffles. "Fascinating," he murmured, as if lost in a reverie. Elsbeth felt moved to prod him out of it.

"The price is twenty crowns," she said, her voice coming out a little too loudly. That was more than he had paid for the three items yesterday combined.

"Is it now?" Mr Persimmon straightened up and looked amused, which annoyed her.

A boy not much older than Elsbeth with a ring in his eyebrow came in carrying a tea tray. "Tea and water," he said without ceremony. He thudded the tray down on the table and walked out.

"Shocking, really, that this place isn't busier," Mr Persimmon said, looking rather forlornly at his mug. Elsbeth could tell from the way the tea had failed to brew that the water was lukewarm. Helping herself to a glass, she took a gulp of water, then, realising how thirsty she was, finished it all.

"Twenty crowns is a good deal of money," Mr

Persimmon resumed.

"The sculpture is from India. Fifteenth century," countered Elsbeth.

"Indeed. To me it seems to have rather more in common with that – what was it? Victorian picture frame you sold me yesterday."

Elsbeth stared at him. So he did know. He knew she was lying. But how much did he know? She found it impossible to read his expression. The moustache was impassive.

A moment passed.

"Still," he continued smoothly, "you know best, I'm sure. I have plenty of clients in Lunden who would be … *very* interested in this item, so my offer to buy anything similar still stands. I will pay the twenty crowns."

Elsbeth took a deep breath in. She had never expected he would actually pay quite so much. Half that amount would have been more than she had hoped for. She tried to keep calm as he delicately drew a leather wallet from his jacket pocket.

"Do you have anything else similar to this?" asked Mr Persimmon, sounding casual.

"Not right now," Elsbeth said. "But I can get more."

"Please do," Mr Persimmon said, and attempted a smile. The moustache did not cooperate, and Elsbeth found herself wondering if he would look less sinister without it.

She looked at his plate. He hadn't touched his food the whole time they had been sitting there.

"Mary's Old Kettle," she said.

"I beg your pardon?"

"I mean, it's a café. It's really good. By the sea. They do sausages and things." She gestured to the burnt toast by way of explanation.

"That is very kind of you. I appreciate the tip," said Mr Persimmon.

She stood up to go, feeling a bit embarrassed.

"If I can offer a tip of my own?" he added.

She paused.

"Be careful."

He took a breath as if about to say more, then stopped himself. The conversation ended on that abrupt note, like a song that had stopped in the middle of the chorus.

But Elsbeth felt lighter and lighter as she walked, then half ran, out of the Seaview Tavern. Twenty crowns! Who cared how much Mr Persimmon knew, if this could help Mum?

Back on the high street, the sun had come out again. The only signs of the storm were the rubbish bins that had been tipped over, with crisp packets and coffee cups lying around in the street. She ran up to her shop and pushed open the door, unable to keep a smile off her face.

"Elsbeth! There you are. I was a bit worried," said Mum, smiling from behind the counter. "That was quite a storm there earlier – I thought you might have been blown over."

"Well, my hair took the brunt of it," said Elsbeth, patting it down again. She knew what it was like – it would be impossible to control until she'd washed it.

"I have hairpins if you need them." Mum didn't meet Elsbeth's eye as she said this, and Elsbeth smiled. Mum knew how Elsbeth felt about hairpins. She put her hand in her pocket, about to show Mum the twenty crowns that Mr Persimmon had given her.

Then she stopped. Where would she tell Mum the money was from? Elsbeth realised she hadn't thought this through. Mum would think it was pretty weird that she had gone to see a customer to sell him something – Elsbeth had never done anything like that before, though she knew that Mum sometimes had private meetings in Lunden at auction houses.

"Yes?" Mum said. She was looking at Elsbeth now, and Elsbeth didn't know what to say. "You know, I noticed there's quite a lot of money in the till," said

Mum. "You must have had a very good day yesterday when I was in Lunden? You didn't say anything at dinner."

Elsbeth gulped. Of course. The money Mr Persimmon had paid yesterday was in the till. It had been more than they normally made in a week. She had to come up with a good reason why. And so, for the first time since she could remember, Elsbeth found herself opening her mouth to say something to Mum that wasn't true.

It wasn't that she had never told a lie. Even to Mum. She'd lost count of the times she'd told Mum that she'd had a nice day at school when she hadn't. But this was different. This wasn't just a breezy answer that would prevent any more questions being asked and stop Mum worrying. Or an answer that left some things out, like not mentioning to Mum that on her walk by the sea she'd also visited some other Somewheres. Lying about where the money came would require imagination and a longer backstory. It would mean she'd have to remember her story and stick to it. It meant she'd have to be devious.

"A group of tourists came in yesterday and bought a few things," Elsbeth heard herself say. Her voice sounded calm. "I forgot to say."

"Well, that's good!" Mum looked pleased, but Elsbeth felt awful. "Maybe they'll tell their friends, and more people will come in."

Elsbeth felt the twenty-crown note in her pocket. She realised she would have to put it in the till when Mum wasn't there and pretend more customers had come in. This wasn't going to be easy.

"Are you OK, Elsbeth? You look worried," said Mum. "Not missing school, surely?"

Elsbeth laughed despite herself. "Nobody misses school, Mum."

"I suppose not!" Mum laughed, and Elsbeth felt happy that she seemed so cheerful. It emboldened her to ask, "What are we going to do, Mum? About the rent this week?"

"Well, I was just going to ask if you wouldn't mind looking after the shop for an hour or so this afternoon?" Mum said. "I thought I might go down to Westbourne to see Lily."

"Lily? At the pawn shop?" Mum and Lily did business together sometimes, when Lily's customers never came to get their things back. Westbourne was a couple of villages away from Lewesby along the coast, and Mum would take the bus there every couple of months or so to see if Lily had any bargains. It was normally family jewels: engagement rings or necklaces from people who needed the money desperately. It made Elsbeth feel sad that they'd had to pawn them. But it didn't seem like the best time to be forking out money for more stuff for the shop. "Don't we… I mean, shouldn't we save our cash for the rent this week?" Elsbeth asked.

Mum winced. "I'm not buying, Elsbeth," she said slowly. "I thought I might … leave a couple of things with Lily."

Pawn jewellery. Elsbeth felt cold. Those families she had felt sorry for – were they now one of those families themselves? "Like, what sort of stuff?"

Mum cleared her throat. "Well, I know my engagement ring would fetch a decent price. Lily has often mentioned it. It's very unusual."

Mum's engagement ring – a hoop of gold with a beautiful golden rose on top and a purple amethyst in the middle. It was the only thing she owned that Dad had given her before he died.

"You can't do that, Mum," said Elsbeth quietly.

"It's the best solution, Elsbeth. It would be enough to get the rent, I'm sure of that."

"And then what? How would you find the money to buy it back?"

"Something will turn up, I'm sure, Elsbeth. Really,

you mustn't worry," said Mum gently.

"Mum, you can't do this," said Elsbeth. To her surprise she realised tears were rolling down her cheeks. "Take something else from the shop. Anything but that."

"Oh, Elsbeth." Mum came out from behind the counter and gave her a hug. "You mustn't cry. We're in a tight spot right now, that's all, but we'll work it out." She hugged Elsbeth tighter. "*I'll* work it out, I mean. You shouldn't be worrying about this. You're only twelve. Sometimes I worry that I treat you too much like a grown-up."

"Mum!" Elsbeth stepped out of the hug. "You don't have to treat me like a child. We always talk about the shop together. I can help you. But you can't pawn your ring."

"Lily specialises in jewellery; you know that," said Mum. "I can hardly offer her a chest of drawers. And she won't take anything that's been on sale at our shop. If we can't sell it, then she probably can't either."

But Elsbeth had already gone to the peacock mirror. She opened a side compartment. In it was a small blue felt bag that looked as if it had marbles inside. She went over to Mum and emptied the contents of the bag in Mum's hand. Two large pearl earrings rolled gently out.

"No, Elsbeth."

"I've never worn them, Mum, and I'm not about to start any time soon."

"You just got your ears pierced."

"I'm twelve, Mum. These are earrings for grown-ups. I'd look like a teacher in them or something."

"You'll be a grown-up someday, Elsbeth. And besides, I thought you wanted to be treated as a grown-up?" Mum smiled, then turned serious. "I can't let you give these away, Elsbeth. They're all I had from my mother."

"Who cut you off because you married Dad," said Elsbeth. "I know the story, Mum. If it's a choice between her earrings and Dad's ring, Dad's ring wins every time. You can't risk losing that." Seeing Mum hesitate, she added, "And that's my final word on the subject."

Then Mum really did laugh, a sound that came from down in her belly, which made Elsbeth feel as if everything was OK with the world again.

"Fine," said Mum. "I promise not to pawn my ring. But I don't promise to pawn your earrings either. I'll go and see Lily anyway to see what she says. Maybe something else will turn up. Now, you should go and make yourself a sandwich. I'll keep an eye on the shop."

But after Elsbeth made a peanut butter sandwich, she didn't sit down to eat it. If Mum was thinking about pawning their jewellery, they were obviously running out of options. Elsbeth needed to sell more things to Mr Persimmon, and she needed them fast. In fact, there was somewhere she could go right now and Mum wouldn't even realise she'd left the house.

She'd go and explore Victoria's Somewhere.

Chapter 5

Elsbeth climbed up the stepladder in the hallway and into the attic. Boxes were scattered about, along with sad, discarded objects that had been taken off the shop floor years ago. A piece of Edwardian lace that had been eaten by moths. An old sewing machine with a broken presser foot. A broken clock, the number three hanging off it like a mouth turned down in disappointment. The doors to the filing cabinet were open and papers lay on the floor – signs that Elsbeth's mum had been in a hurry yesterday before she went to the bank.

Elsbeth looked at the opening by the window seat. The one where it had all begun two years ago. She had thought for ages that there was something special about the attic that allowed her to go to Nowhere. But then something had happened at school, right before the summer holidays.

She had had to take a maths exam. They were all sat in the school's huge damp hall, filled with sniffling kids. She'd been trying to focus on triangles and closed her eyes to remember the formula. It had a lot of letters in it. She had started to see it on the page in front of her when the energy surge came again. It shimmered around her, daring her to go in. She'd realised that she was sitting right on top of an opening. But this time Elsbeth knew not to move. The thought of escaping her maths exam was very appealing, but when she imagined how everyone would react if Elsbeth Tawney evaporated in the exam hall she knew she couldn't do it. She moved on to some easier sums and the feeling faded. That was when she realised that openings were all over the place. In the local butcher's, in the loos at school, on the beach and even walking along the high street. She just had to pay attention. Then, once she let the energy rise, the opening would let her through.

It was only when a customer in the shop noticed a bracelet she was wearing that Victoria had given her and asked where she had bought it, that she realised this was an opportunity. She hadn't sold the bracelet

– it had been a gift, after all – but the customer had offered her a lot of money for it. So she'd started going further into Nowhere. And the empty houses by the sea had seemed like a good place to start.

It had never really occurred to Elsbeth that she might leave Lewesby when she was older, like so many other kids at school said they wanted to do. Mum had often told her how hard it had been to start the shop from nothing and to make friends with the locals. How important it was to feel settled. Elsbeth would inherit the shop one day; she knew that. Her life was all mapped out for her. And on one level Elsbeth didn't know what she was missing: she and Mum didn't go on holidays to Lunden or Normandy, like some of the kids in her class did. They couldn't afford it – and besides, as Mum always said, they lived in a place that other people wanted to *come* to on holiday. Lewesby was in all the history books. Tourists came from all over the world to wander down the quaint old cobbled streets.

So going to the Somewheres was the first time Elsbeth had ever gone anywhere really different. It was like her little quiet, secret rebellion.

She went over to the attic window and closed her eyes. It always felt the same. A sort of humming came over her, then a rising feeling, like energy was moving through her body and coming out of the top of her head. She suddenly felt lighter and went very still, focusing on the energy. The air around her body took on a different quality, like it was listening to her. Then the sucking feeling came, and she stepped into Nowhere.

Victoria's Somewhere was easy to get to: one large step to the left. She'd been there hundreds of times. There were a couple of Somewheres in between, Elsbeth knew that. She'd come out in empty attics before that weren't quite right. So Victoria had put a doll's head on a nail sticking out of the attic wall so that Elsbeth would know she was in the right place. It summed up Victoria's attitude to dolls.

Elsbeth wondered if Victoria would be there. She'd been up in the attic less and less recently. Her parents had been sending her to stay with her grandparents, as it wasn't safe by the sea in her Somewhere. She thought about the flooded houses she'd been in yesterday. One of those had been in Victoria's Somewhere, she was sure. She just hoped it wasn't the one with the huge wave.

As soon as she stepped out of the kaleidoscope, she knew something was different. The doll's head was still there – eyeless, its unbrushed hair at right angles to its head – but most of the boxes that filled the attic were gone, though some still lay around half opened. It looked as if someone had been packing in a hurry.

It was the same when she peeped out of the trapdoor. Victoria's house was laid out a bit differently to Elsbeth's, and the stepladder led directly down to her bedroom. But Victoria's things were gone – her toys, her clothes, the pictures of her friends on the walls. There was one old teddy left, with a missing eye, under the bed. Elsbeth picked it up. She couldn't see Mr Persimmon paying good money for this.

Then she heard a crash in the street. She went to the window. But her eye was drawn to the sea line. The waves had come halfway up Victoria's town. Some of the houses by the cliff were under water. They were the houses where she'd been yesterday, she realised. It was hard to tell, but it didn't seem like this was the Somewhere with the huge wave that was about to destroy everything. It still didn't look good, though. She was glad Victoria had got away.

Elsbeth opened a few drawers quickly, half wondering if Victoria had left her a note to say goodbye, but there was nothing there. Victoria had always been neat, seeming to actually enjoy stacking toys in order and putting them away when they'd finished playing with them. She'd probably packed all her things to take wherever she was going, even if she had been in a rush. Elsbeth decided she might have better luck downstairs.

She went out into the narrow hallway. It was lined with empty squares on the walls where the pictures had been. A lantern was still hanging over the staircase and she studied it. It was made of copper-like metal. It might not be worth much if she'd found it at home but the fact it was from a Somewhere might double its value. But she could see the reason the family hadn't taken it with them, particularly if they'd left in a hurry. You couldn't reach the lantern from the landing or the staircase – it would require a stepladder. Or possibly – Elsbeth took a closer look – she could balance some sort of board across the banisters to stand on and reach it. She decided to go downstairs and see if there was anything like that in the broom cupboard.

Then she heard a creak.

It sounded like someone had put their foot on a floorboard and then frozen. Elsbeth went very still. It had come from behind her – from Victoria's room. That meant her opening in the attic was blocked off. There was bound to be another opening somewhere. But if she ran away, she wouldn't get the lantern. She racked her brain. Did Victoria have a cat? She didn't think so. Elsbeth told herself it was probably nothing, to calm her thumping heart. But she should check to make sure. She tiptoed towards Victoria's bedroom door then summoned all her strength to shout loudly. "Who's there?" She flung the door open as she shouted.

There was a sort of squawking sound, and she found herself face to face with a boy who was cowering as if she were about to hit him.

But this wasn't just any boy, Elsbeth realised. It was the boy from this morning. The one who had helped her with the statue. It was the same black messy hair, and those charcoal eyes with white specks, which looked like a starry night sky. He was a year or so younger than she was, Elsbeth judged, and Mum would have said he needed feeding up. The other-worldliness of the midnight eyes was offset by his chin, which jutted out in a rather defiant way.

"You!" she said in shock. This wasn't the same Somewhere as the one with the sculpture. How had he been there, then here? Had he got lost in Nowhere after all, and come out here by mistake?

"Oh, er, hello." The boy straightened up awkwardly. "Fancy seeing you here." He tried to laugh, but it came out as a choke.

He seemed very embarrassed, and Elsbeth stared at

him with a dawning realisation.

"Are you ... *following* me?"

The boy stared back at her. Elsbeth saw him take a breath to deny it, then realise it was hopeless.

"Yes," he said. "I'm sorry." He flinched again, waiting for her reaction.

But it hadn't occurred to Elsbeth to be angry. "*How?*" she simply said. It seemed a hugely important question – even more than why he was following her, or what they were doing there together. And it was a question she'd never really asked herself before either.

The boy shrugged, taking the question at face value. "The same way you do. I saw you take that letter opener last week. I wanted to get that myself. My grandmother would have killed for it." He said this last part with a strange intensity.

The letter opener that Mr Persimmon had bought for a tidy sum. This brought Elsbeth back to the present moment with a bump. Was this boy her competition? Her eyes narrowed. "So why didn't you take it?"

The boy looked at the floor again and shifted his weight. "I ... I lose things. When I go through. I don't know how you do it," he said, suddenly looking up at her and fixing his star-speckled eyes on her like a torch. "I've never seen anything like it. Transportation is very advanced. People usually can't do it as well as you. Certainly not at our age."

Elsbeth stared at him. She had no idea what he was talking about. "Our age – how old are you?" she asked.

"I'm almost twelve," he said to Elsbeth's surprise. Just a few months younger than her.

There was a crash outside and they both jumped. Broken glass. Voices shouted "Over here!" followed by hasty footsteps from more than one person. She'd heard these sounds in this Somewhere yesterday, she remembered, down at the houses by the sea. She understood what was happening here now. Everyone had left their homes because of the sea moving in, and looters had come in to scavenge what they could find. Elsbeth looked at the boy and made a quick decision.

"Look, we may not have much time. I want to get that lantern. Can you help me? I know you helped me before," she said, seeing his look. "But then I'll definitely owe you. I can try to help you with – er – Transportation, maybe."

"OK." The boy nodded and padded over to the banister to size up the situation. "My name's Idris, by the way."

"Elsbeth."

To her surprise he sprang on to the banister and, in a

motion like a dancer, balanced one hand on the ceiling while leaning perilously over the staircase to reach the lantern with the other.

"You'll fall," hissed Elsbeth. But he was already deftly unhooking the lantern. It wobbled as it came off, but he caught it neatly and swung backwards at the same time, only shaking the floorboards a bit with his dismount.

"Impressive."

Idris smiled. But at that moment the front door downstairs swung open and a tall scraggy-looking man with a half-grown beard and a hunted look in his eyes appeared. He stared straight up at them. "Live ones!" he shouted, and made for the stairs.

Elsbeth didn't want to think about what he meant by that. They both ran, Elsbeth dragging Idris towards the ladder in Victoria's room. But the man was fast and as they started climbing the ladder Idris shrieked. She looked down to see the man had grabbed the boy's trouser leg and was dragging him back down. She tried to help him up but the man was stronger than her.

There was only one thing to do. Elsbeth lifted the lantern and threw it down at the man with all her strength. It hit his head with a nasty clang and he fell back.

"Come on!" She pulled Idris up – he was surprisingly heavy – and half dragged him towards the opening in the attic. She glanced back in a panic. The man had recovered quickly and was already at the top of the ladder. She saw a flash of a nasty cut that had streaked across his forehead.

But Elsbeth was too quick for him. They were already at the opening, which hadn't yet sealed itself up. As the looter lunged forward, she and Idris threw themselves backwards.

And, just like that, they were together in Nowhere.

Chapter 6

The kaleidoscope glowed like an aquarium, the coloured lights in front of them like little sparkling green and purple fish as they stood in the darkness. The air was as thick as treacle.

Elsbeth held her breath for a second, glancing around to make sure the looter hadn't somehow fallen into Nowhere too. But it was clear there was nobody else here. She glanced at Idris. The light from the kaleidoscope danced across his face. She had never seen anyone else in Nowhere. They were surrounded by darkness – it was as if they weren't real, or shouldn't be there.

Elsbeth tried to think what to do. She'd lost that lantern after throwing it at the looter and now she was empty-handed. This hadn't been part of her plan. She'd just wanted to get new things for Mr Persimmon, and now she was standing in Nowhere with a strange boy who could do what she could and seemed to be from a different Somewhere altogether. The question was: could she trust him? She knew nothing about him, after all.

Then Elsbeth had that sinking feeling again. The floor felt like it was rising over her toes.

"We need to move," said Idris, obviously feeling the same thing.

Elsbeth knew she had to make a decision. She wasn't taking Idris back to her Somewhere. That was too risky. But she wasn't going to give up on her plan to find something new to sell to Mr Persimmon either. So she took two large steps to the right, moving past her Somewhere. *That should do it*, she thought. "Come on then," she said to him, and they went through together into a new Somewhere.

The first things Elsbeth saw were the cliffs and the sea out of the window, and for a second she thought they were back in her attic. But this was a different one. Boxes were stacked neatly like Lego blocks, all the same size, with none of the mess that her attic at home had. She peered at them. They might have something worth taking in them, she supposed. But now that they were safely out of Nowhere, she needed to talk to Idris properly.

She gave him her firmest stare. "How long were you following me?"

Idris shifted awkwardly. "A week, maybe."

A week! Elsbeth thought back to the times she'd been in other Somewheres. It did explain a funny feeling she'd had – a sort of prickling at the back of her neck from time to time. "How did you even find me? And where are you from? Are you from that Somewhere where I took the sculpture from?"

"I'm a lot further away from home than that," Idris said. "The thing is, I sort of ran away. That is, I didn't run away exactly, but I'm supposed to be able to Transport, and my grandmother said I shouldn't come home until I'd worked it out. We had a fight about it."

He sighed. "I'm a disappointment to her. She tells me that all the time. I'm supposed to be able to Transport small things by now. My mum – her daughter – could do it, and my other mum too, although she wasn't as good. So I should be able to. But I don't have the gift."

Elsbeth looked at him curiously. "So what we can do is … normal, where you come from?"

"Not normal exactly. It's quite rare, and those

that have the ability are much sought after. Though everyone in my family usually has it and we're sort of special, I suppose. But I'm guessing people don't know about it in your Sphere."

"No." Elsbeth couldn't imagine it. Not having to hide what you could do from everyone.

"Anyway, I'm sure that's why my grandmother took me in after my parents died."

Elsbeth held her breath. But Idris continued swiftly.

"She thought I'd be of use to her one day. She has a rather large operation, I guess you'd say. And I'm turning out not to be of any use at all. That's why she told me I had to go out and learn. She thought not being able to go back home might be an incentive. Sometimes I wonder if it really is." Idris gave a half-laugh.

Elsbeth paused. Her dad had died, but that was before she was born. She hadn't known him. She couldn't imagine losing Mum now – losing both parents was unimaginable. Saying she was sorry sounded too flat in her head, and she couldn't bring herself to form the words.

"Wouldn't she take you in anyway because you're her grandson?" she asked carefully.

"Ha! She only wanted me because she thought I was

worth something. That's all people are to her. Everyone has to earn their keep – she says that all the time. But I can't Transport anything. I've tried and I simply can't. I just come out and it's gone. My grandmother got furious about it and, trust me, you don't want to be on the wrong side of her."

There was something funny and formal about the way Idris said "my grandmother". Not "Gran" or "Grandma" like other kids did. As if it were her title or something.

"Can't you just put something in your pocket?" Elsbeth asked. "I don't see how it could fall out on the way if you did that."

"It doesn't work like that," Idris said with a sigh. "I've tried everything, believe me. Anything that isn't from my place seems to just … dissolve in the place between the Spheres. It's even happened with clothes. One time I arrived back with nothing on at all as I had to change my clothes in another Sphere – I had an accident with a pig."

Elsbeth looked down at the floor quickly at this. She had that awful feeling of being about to turn red, and she didn't want Idris to see it. "What do we do now then?" she asked, changing the subject.

Idris looked at her hopefully. "We could help each

other. I need to Transport things and you're stealing stuff for a reason, aren't you? I could help you with that. I can take you to some good places, even if I can't carry anything back." His midnight eyes shone at her and crinkled at the edges when he smiled. This grandmother had to be made of strong stuff, Elsbeth thought, if this was how he turned on the charm.

"How long will it take, teaching you Transportation? I don't have much time, you see. I need to get stuff to sell in my shop" – instinct made Elsbeth decide not to tell Idris about Mr Persimmon – "and we're behind on the rent. The landlord said he'll kick us out if we don't pay it by the end of the week."

Idris blew air through his teeth. It wasn't an unsympathetic sound. "You are in a pickle," he said. He studied the boxes stacked in front of them for a minute. "How about this? Forget helping me for now – I'll help you until you pay the landlord. Once he's got the money, the pressure is off, then you return the favour and help me with Transportation."

Elsbeth frowned at him. Was there a catch? They were negotiating, and Mum said you never got something for nothing. But he thought he would learn to Transport, and he had time. It made sense from his side, she supposed. The problem was she had no idea how to teach someone how to do what she did, and very much doubted that she could.

He doesn't need to know that, a voice in her head said. *And you need to find stuff to sell to Mr Persimmon.*

"Fine," she said quickly. "It's a deal."

Idris looked thrilled and put out his hand to shake on it. But honesty got the better of Elsbeth as she extended hers in return and she found herself saying, "I don't know if I'll be able to teach you, though. I don't know how I'm doing it myself."

But Idris didn't seem to care. "You're so good at it," he said breezily. "I'm sure you'll be able to help me."

They each thought they had the better deal, she thought. That was probably the best possible outcome in a negotiation.

"Well, seeing as we're here, shall we have a look in these boxes?" she asked.

Idris glanced around, as if someone might be listening. "Never a good idea to stay too long in HostTech," he remarked. He examined one of the boxes, running his fingers over the sides. "They're taped up pretty strongly."

"I've got a penknife." Elsbeth pulled it out of her pocket, and cut down the side of one marked TELOS, 0–6 MONTHS, which didn't sound hugely promising. A pile of baby clothes spilled out. They looked decidedly normal. "I don't think I could sell these," she said.

"What about this one?" Idris had picked up one of the smaller boxes. He rattled it. "Sounds more substantial."

Elsbeth cut it open. Inside were some tin boxes. She opened the lid of one and a ballerina popped up. A song Elsbeth didn't recognise played, and the ballerina started to twirl. She smiled. She'd had one of these when she was little.

Or maybe not. After a couple more twirls, the ballerina stepped daintily out of the box and continued dancing across the attic floor. Elsbeth watched it, mesmerised.

"Look at these!" breathed Idris. He had opened another tin box. A group of soldiers were clambering over the side and hopping briskly to the ground. They marched along then stood to attention in front of one who was clearly the leader.

"What … what are they?" whispered Elsbeth. "Is it magic?"

Idris snorted. "Solar-powered, more like." He glanced at the attic window, which was letting in a muted light. "Or maybe some limited form of artificial intelligence. This HostTech isn't one of the more advanced ones, though."

The ballerina had immersed herself in what Elsbeth thought was called a pirouette. A couple of the soldiers were looking sideways at her as she twirled. Then there was a disapproving metallic crunching sound from their leader and they snapped their heads back to the front. Idris had used that odd word again. "HostTech?" she said, her eyes still on the ballerina.

"The name of this series," Idris said. He saw Elsbeth's look of confusion. "My tutors were always banging on about this. If you come from a trading family, you have to know this stuff. All the Spheres are in a series. This one is in HostTech. Stands for hostile technology. I'm pretty sure this is the same one that you stole the sculpture from." He looked around the attic. "Just a different bit of it. Obviously."

Elsbeth remembered the thumb plate that the man had used, and the cameras like eyes on stalks in the streets. But these dancing toys didn't seem hostile. Or were the soldiers about to start shooting them?

As if he could tell what she was thinking, Idris added, "It doesn't mean all the technology is bad. Just that that's the general theme of the Sphere. And then the series before this one is HostNat, where we just came from."

"Victoria's Somewhere," said Elsbeth. "Where the sea

is rising." She remembered the different Somewheres she'd got stuck in at the houses by the coast, where the sea was at different levels in each place. HostNat: hostile nature. Those must all have been HostNat Spheres at different stages. She frowned. "So which one is mine? HostTech or HostNat?"

"Your Sphere is like my Sphere. It's balanced. Sometimes you get those in between series of Spheres. It means there isn't any one force dominating them. Usually it means they're quite quiet."

That makes sense, thought Elsbeth. If there was one thing Lewesby was, it was quiet. Maybe that explained the restless feeling she had there these days. She looked down at the ballerina and the tin soldiers. "Can we take these then? Won't they mind? The toys, I mean?"

Idris laughed. "They're not people. They just look real. Bet they're running on some very basic programming." He reached down and put a soldier in his pocket. "See?" He held out the still pocket to Elsbeth. "It's stopped moving."

Elsbeth approached the ballerina, feeling nervous. The ballerina continued twirling and didn't look up even when Elsbeth reached her hand towards her. As soon as she picked her up, the ballerina went stiff, like a mouse playing dead. She put it in her pocket and looked at Idris. "Well, this is a good haul."

"You need to take the soldiers, though," said Idris. "I'll just lose them when we go back to the place between Spheres."

"We wouldn't want that, would we?"

They both swung round, startled. A man in a gold suit stood in the doorway, an unpleasant smirk on his face. His clothes reminded Elsbeth of the silver-suited man who had owned the shop where she'd taken the sculpture from. This was obviously how people dressed in this Somewhere. This man could have been the silver-suited man's brother – the cruel expression on their faces was just the same. Elsbeth's hand went unconsciously to her wrist, where a bruise had formed since the morning.

Idris was already edging towards the opening. Elsbeth moved towards him, keeping her eyes on the man. Yet he stood just outside the room, looking strangely relaxed. He didn't look as if he were about to pounce on them.

"Go!" shouted Idris, and they both leaped for the opening. Elsbeth had a flash of the man standing there, calmly watching them. *Why isn't he reacting?* But instead of being in the darkness of Nowhere, she and Idris were still in the man's attic. Worse, she couldn't feel the opening at all.

"I don't know where you think you're going," the man said. "You can't climb out of the window. I turned the perimeter boundary on as soon as I heard you. The Polit will be here soon." He said this as if he were talking about the weather.

Elsbeth had no idea what a perimeter boundary was. But whatever it was, it wasn't just stopping them from getting out of the window. Now that she looked at the man more closely, she could see faint pink lines in front of him. She took a step closer. The room was humming.

"A force field," said Idris. He frowned. "And it must be stopping the openings working too. Well, we can wait."

Could they? Elsbeth wasn't so sure. There were clearly a lot of rules in this Somewhere. She didn't like the sound of the Polit either. She remembered how the silver man had pressed her thumb on to a metal plate. Her eyes darted to the doorway and froze as she saw this room had one too.

There was a clatter on the staircase and three men with helmets covering their entire faces appeared. "Polit!" barked one.

They could have been robots for all Elsbeth could see of them. There was no skin on display anywhere –

rubber covered their hands and feet, and the helmets extended down past the neck.

"Prints!" barked another. The third marched into the room – it didn't break the pink lines, as Elsbeth briefly hoped – and grabbed her and Idris. He pulled them roughly over to the metal plate. When he pressed Idris's thumb on to it, it triggered the red flashing UNKNOWN, just as hers had last time.

"What does that mean?" the gold man said.

The Polit ignored him. Her thumb was next.

It beeped. REGISTERED OFFENDER. Elsbeth's heart sank. So it was the exact same Somewhere she'd been in this morning. The Somewhere she'd stolen the sculpture from. The sound was even louder than it had been for Idris. The system must have stored her prints.

"Cuffs," grunted the first one, who seemed to be the leader. They were not men – if they were men – of many words.

Elsbeth's and Idris's hands were roughly twisted behind their backs. She felt a steely *click* of handcuffs fastening together, a further setback to any hope of escape. Then they were marched down the staircase to the front door. The robot men's long black guns clattered carelessly down the walls, knocking a couple of pictures off and smashing them on the ground.

"Hey! Careful there," called the gold man.

One of the robot men turned and stared at him.

"I mean, don't worry. It's no trouble," the gold man added hastily.

"Bet he regrets calling them now," muttered Idris, sparking a "Silence!"

Elsbeth tried to make eye contact with Idris as they were dragged into the sunlight of the street outside but he seemed to have gone smaller, turning in on himself as if he thought nobody would notice him like that. She saw they were headed towards a van. Movement was the last thing they needed – they'd never be near an opening for long enough to get through. As Idris said, they'd just have to wait.

Elsbeth caught a glimpse of the cameras, like eyes on stalks, swivelling towards them before she was shoved into the van. She and Idris sat on benches facing each other. With a queasy feeling, Elsbeth saw that there was nobody in the driver's seat. The steering wheel moved by itself. A robot car. The guards stared straight ahead as they set off, rattling along.

It didn't feel real. Only half an hour ago Elsbeth had stood in Nowhere, free to make choices. Now she was losing control. She dug her nails into her palms. Unfortunately this was very real. She tried desperately to think. She should say something to these guards, though there didn't seem much point. But Mum always said you should show strength in negotiations even if you were in a weak position. People admired strength. She did her best to feel that her adult mask was on and her voice came out a little too loudly.

"Where are we going?"

But there was only silence. These guards obviously weren't in the negotiation business.

They came to a stop, the engine running. Perhaps they were at a traffic light – there were no windows, so it was hard to tell. She looked up to see Idris staring at her, the corners of his eyes twitching. She frowned at him. Had he been trying to tell her something? The van set off again and he let out an annoyed clicking sound.

They drove on and on. Then, suddenly, there was silence outside. What little light had come in from the front window had gone. The van stopped. For a second Elsbeth wondered if there was time to feel for an opening. Perhaps that was what Idris had been doing the last time they stopped. But the guard dragged them out too quickly. They emerged into a cold, damp darkness. Elsbeth was sure they were underground, but there wasn't much time to look around. They were pulled onward. The guard holding Idris led the way, the second followed with Elsbeth and the third brought up the rear. Then they were frogmarched through a dark tunnel with overhead lamps that buzzed with a low light.

Idris made a break for freedom. Elsbeth let out a cry as he scuffled with the guard holding him, escaped his grip and threw himself at the wall ahead of him. But if he'd felt an opening he wasn't fast enough. His guard yanked him back by the handcuffs, making him yelp. Elsbeth was pushed aside by the third guard, who strode forward and snapped, "Enough." He produced a long metal rod from his jacket and hit Idris over the head. He went limp instantly.

Elsbeth stared at his unmoving body. "Idris." Her voice came out sounding small, and the guard next to her gave her a casual push, a warning not to say anything more.

The other guard pulled Idris's unresponsive body up. He dragged him to a door in the side of the tunnel and shoved him inside. Elsbeth could barely breathe as the guard jerked her forward. She had brought Idris here. What had she done?

They came to a second door and Elsbeth was pushed through.

A guard yanked the handcuffs off her. She rubbed at her wrists as she looked around the room. She was in what looked like a silver metal box and for a moment she felt like the ballerina in her pocket. The bright lights above her head buzzed and flickered, making her wince. A smell like rotting sports shoes came from a corner – the only part of the room not covered in metal plates.

The door slammed and Elsbeth swung round. She was alone.

Chapter 7

The first thing Elsbeth did was pace the room, looking for an opening. Right over the foul-smelling hole in the ground that clearly passed for a toilet, she felt the familiar energy. It *would* have to be there, she thought. The good thing was that there didn't seem to be a force field in the prison cell – probably because the metal door was so thick it was hard to imagine anyone ever being able to break out. She couldn't see any pink lines, and apart from the buzzing of the lights overhead she didn't hear any humming sound like the one in the gold man's attic.

Her first instinct was to leave straight away. The problem was Idris. How could she leave without him, now that the guards had knocked him out? On the one hand, she was fairly sure he could look after himself. His escape attempt in the corridor must have been because he felt an opening. If he had been willing to leave Elsbeth to fight her own way out, surely she shouldn't have any qualms about doing the same?

On the other hand, Elsbeth felt it was her fault that he was even here. Idris had warned her it wasn't safe, but she'd been too focused on taking something back for the shop. And besides, she could hardly just leave Idris in some underground dungeon. He didn't deserve to be here. She looked around the room again. *No one* did.

A voice suddenly filled the room. "Processing! Fifteen minutes!" it boomed from the ceiling. Then there was silence again.

Elsbeth did not fancy finding out what processing might involve. That meant she had fifteen minutes to figure out what to do. Idris was in the next cell, but probably still passed out. What if he hadn't woken up by the time they were processed? They might get separated, then she wouldn't be able to find him. She knocked on the metal-plated wall. Silence. She rattled the door without any real hope she could get it open. This was a Somewhere that did things properly.

Then it came to her. The opening. She couldn't get

into Idris's cell in *this* Somewhere, but maybe she could in *another*.

Somewheres close by to each other were usually similar, Elsbeth knew. From her attic she could get to other attics, like Victoria's. So it made sense that a Somewhere next to this one would probably also have prison cells in the same place.

That wouldn't be much help. But if she went to a Somewhere a bit further away, she might find a Somewhere that didn't have prison cells. Then she could walk to where Idris's cell would be – about ten large strides, she calculated – look for an opening to go back into Nowhere, and then come back out in this Somewhere, but in Idris's cell. Then they could escape together. Of course, it would depend on there being an opening in Idris's cell. But it was worth a shot.

She approached the hole in the ground, holding her breath so she didn't have to smell what had clearly not been cleaned out since the last poor person had been stuck in the cell. She closed her eyes and stepped through into Nowhere.

The relief of being free was overwhelming. She stared at the kaleidoscope and exhaled slowly. The guards couldn't get her here. She was safe. But not for long. She had to go back and save Idris. At least it was easier to think now that she wasn't in immediate danger.

The question was how far to go in Nowhere. She didn't want to end up in another cell. Who knew who might be in there with her? And the whole point of this was to get to a Somewhere where she could walk beyond the physical space of her cell. Too far, on the other hand, and she might lose her bearings. A few Somewheres away was probably the best option. Elsbeth slowly moved around the kaleidoscope, measuring her steps and keeping an eye on the colours. She'd try about five Somewheres away from where she had left, she decided.

But when she tried to step out into the new Somewhere, she couldn't move. Her hands met something solid. She pushed and nothing happened. She felt something squidgy and drew her hand back in disgust. A worm. She was under the earth.

But not quite under. The earth was in front of her like a wall, and she could feel Nowhere just behind her. She was not fully in this Somewhere, it seemed. The earth was preventing her from stepping out properly. It would have been like being buried alive, Elsbeth thought with a shudder as she went back to Nowhere. But she felt a pang of concern. The prison cells had been underground, so if other Somewheres didn't have prison cells, they might just have earth. Would they all be like this?

The next two Somewheres were the same – earth, smelling wetter and saltier each time, maybe because the sea was above the ground in those places. She decided to go back the other way. At this rate she might end up in the sea. She remembered the booming voice in the cell. It might not feel real in the kaleidoscope, but it was very real for Idris. She was running out of time. She had to save him.

She hit earth a couple more times, then was briefly back in her cell. But the next opening allowed her out. Her feet struck something hard. She could tell she was in a huge space. Her breath seemed to echo. It was dark. She strained her eyes.

It was an underground car park. Perfect.

Elsbeth looked down. She was standing in an empty parking space. She looked to her right. Idris's cell in the HostTech Somewhere would be about three parking spaces away, she thought. But that space wasn't empty. A red sports car sat there, sleek and smug. She paced round the car to find an opening near it. Nothing. Then, at the side door, she felt the energy. But this wasn't the centre of the opening – not quite. She stretched out her arm, and realised it was stronger over the roof of the car. In fact, the car was parked on the opening that would get her into Idris's cell.

She couldn't waste time. She glanced around. A woman on the other side of the car park was wheeling a trolley filled with bags. Elsbeth peered at her. She could have sworn it was their neighbour from across the street: Mrs Laplan, who lived above the butcher's. Had she ended up in her own Somewhere, Elsbeth wondered? She had barely paid attention to the colours in Nowhere when she'd been in there. But there wasn't time to think about that now.

Checking the woman wasn't looking her way, Elsbeth held on to the ridge on the red car's roof and pulled herself up, using the wing mirror as a foothold.

Her foot slipped and she looked down to see the mirror hanging at an awkward angle. *Whoever bought this car can afford to get it fixed*, she thought to herself. She closed her eyes, praying that nobody had noticed her. The opening fizzled, prickling her skin, and she went into Nowhere.

If that had been her Somewhere, Elsbeth thought, then that meant that the HostTech one where Idris was in prison was just next door – only to the right, not the left, like Victoria's Somewhere. She'd obviously got confused. She took one careful step to the right and went forward.

She exhaled with relief as she came out of the opening to see Idris lying on the ground in a room that looked identical to the cell she'd been locked up in. Her plan had worked. Elsbeth realised she had been digging her nails into her palms and she released them now, feeling pain for the first time.

The hideous smell was stronger. She looked down. She was standing in the hole in the ground in Idris's cell.

Elsbeth yelped and leaped to the side, scuffing her shoes in the dirt to try to get the smell – and whatever else might have been in the hole – off them.

Idris stirred. "What? Who?" he slurred, lifting his head off the floor.

They didn't have much time, Elsbeth knew. Processing, whatever that was, would be happening any minute now. Sure enough, she heard feet stomping along outside and a banging at the cell next door. "Processing!" barked a guard's voice. Keys rattled, and she heard a cell door being unlocked. *Her* cell door.

"We have to go!" Elsbeth rushed over to Idris and pulled him up.

Next door, voices were shouting. A whistle blew.

The guard had realised she was gone. She shook Idris. "Hurry!" He stood up, a little wobbly, and she pulled him towards the opening. But before they got there an alarm sounded from the ceiling – a short, sharp honking sound that hurt her ears. There was a buzz, and Elsbeth realised with horror that the walls of Idris's cell were flickering pink. The guard had turned on the perimeter boundary.

If the perimeter boundary was on, the opening wouldn't work. Elsbeth stared as a key started rattling in Idris's cell door.

"What's going on?" Idris whispered. He seemed more alert now, and Elsbeth could feel how tense he was.

They were trapped. The guards would take them away. Worse, they would know that she could escape, so they would make sure the perimeter boundary was always on. She would never be able to find another opening. She might be stuck here forever. What about Mum, and home?

The alarm had been getting louder and louder, and it now felt as if it were coming from inside Elsbeth herself. She looked down at Idris. He was saying something, but no sound seemed to be coming out. She looked back up. The door was open now and the guard was standing there, pointing a gun at them and shouting something, but Elsbeth couldn't hear it. She felt very still. She realised that the ground underneath her was shaking. A piece of metal fell from the ceiling and hit the guard on the foot. He dropped his gun and howled. Elsbeth stared at him as if it had happened in slow motion.

Then she realised that all around her the energy was rising. An opening. That was odd. There was another one after all, right where she was standing, and she could reach it even though the perimeter boundary was on. Holding tightly on to Idris, she stepped back into it, as the ground began to shake further. The guard raised his gun towards them, but then fell backwards, firing over their heads. The last thing Elsbeth saw before they were sucked into Nowhere was the shocked look in his eyes.

◆

"Um, Elsbeth," Idris said as they stood in Nowhere together. But he didn't finish whatever he was trying to say. They were standing in silence, their hearts thumping in their chests, letting the sound of relief fill their ears.

"We should go," said Elsbeth. She felt stunned. What had just happened? It had felt different, when the energy rose. More powerful. And more out of control. "They can't follow us in here, can they?"

"I don't think so," said Idris. "That wasn't a sophisticated HostTech Sphere. But some of them do know how to travel."

"Well, let's not risk it." Elsbeth took a careful step to the left, to where her Somewhere was. She didn't fancy taking her chances anywhere else right now. She was going to have to take Idris back with her after all. She reminded herself that she knew very little about him. And he had been following her all that time. But he had tried to help her. Twice. She took hold of Idris's arm firmly and stepped through the opening.

They came out into the underground car park together. Elsbeth sized it up in more detail this time, to check it really was her Somewhere. The style of the number plates was familiar. Thinking about it, she was sure this was the big supermarket on the outskirts of town that she and Mum came to once a month. That meant there was a bus station just outside. An underground prison in HostTech was just an underground carpark here. She heard the wind howling above them. The storm was back again.

"Elsbeth," said Idris slowly. "Do you know what happened back there?"

"Oh, I worked out how to get into your cell by going back into Nowhere," said Elsbeth.

"Not that," said Idris. "When we escaped. The perimeter boundary was still on, you know."

Elsbeth frowned. "No, they must have turned it off. Otherwise how did we get out?"

"That's my point," said Idris. "How *did* we get out?"

The car park started to shake and Elsbeth gasped. It was as if they were back in the cell again. What was going on?

"This is your Somewhere, isn't it? Do you get earthquakes here?" Idris was strangely calm.

"N-no!" Elsbeth's teeth chattered. "We're not in the right part of the world for it."

"Well, we get them at home a lot. This one isn't too bad. You just have to not panic. Stand in a doorway." Idris took Elsbeth's arm to lead her to the doorway at the stairwell nearby. By the time they were there the ground was steady again.

Elsbeth took a deep breath. For a minute it had felt like the Somewheres were leaking into each other. That the underground car park would somehow morph into the cell and they'd be prisoners again. She shook herself. That didn't make sense. Maybe she was travelling too much. "Come on," she said to Idris, and they went towards the car park exit, which brought them to the bus stop outside the supermarket. A few people with shopping bags stood there, talking at each other animatedly. Elsbeth assumed they knew each other, then realised they were talking about the storm that had just passed.

"Those hail stones! Never seen anything like it."

"Dented that windscreen over there."

"I thought I'd get blown over."

Below them stood the harbour. Grey clouds were beating a hasty retreat across the horizon, and Elsbeth saw boats lurched on their sides. People were throwing ropes to haul them the right way back up.

"A hailstorm and an earthquake at the same time," murmured Idris. "Is that normal?"

"No," said Elsbeth. She remembered the huge wave that she'd seen in the other Somewhere, heading towards the coast, about to destroy everything. Was that going to happen here too? Was this somehow her fault?

"That opening, Elsbeth," said Idris. "I could have sworn it wasn't there before. We were standing there and I didn't feel a thing, then suddenly it was there. It felt … different, you know?"

It had felt different. Usually when she felt an opening it was like walking into a cool breeze. This was more like the cool breeze was coming from her. Like she was the wind.

"Maybe it was the force field," she said uncertainly. "That made it all feel different, I suppose?"

Idris was looking at the boats overturned in the harbour. "Hmm."

The bus arrived and they were jostled by the shoppers into the seats. She put her hand in her pocket. The ballerina was still there. It felt cold and metallic, not alive at all. Idris must have been right. It was just a sophisticated form of robot. "Do you still have the soldier?" she asked Idris.

Idris felt his pocket. "Drat! It's gone, of course. You should have taken it off me."

Elsbeth felt slightly irked at this. "Right, because I wasn't busy enough saving you from that prison cell."

A shopper stared over his shoulder at them and Elsbeth smiled back at him, rolling her eyes as if she'd just made a joke.

Idris shivered. "Is it winter here?"

Elsbeth laughed. "It's August. The height of summer. Why, are you cold?"

But Idris was being serious. "You must be joking. It's freezing," he said. "You'd better have some warm clothes at yours."

The coastal path back to Lewesby was difficult for the bus to navigate – the storm had blown branches on to the road, and the driver had to get out a couple of times and move them. When they reached the high street at last, Elsbeth could finally see the full extent of the storm damage. Tables and chairs that had been set up in the street for tourists were overturned, and waiters were hastily putting them back in the right place. Some of the side streets were unpassable, flooded ankle-deep. Elsbeth saw tourists turning away, muttering to themselves crossly about the infrastructure of these seaside towns.

But when they reached Elsbeth's shop, the damage looked even worse. The glass front door had been smashed in. Had something flown at it in the height of the storm? The door was unlocked, and Elsbeth pushed it open. The shop was in disarray. A lamp lay smashed on the floor.

Worst of all, there was no Mum at the counter.

Elsbeth rushed over. Had they been burgled? She hit the open button on the cash machine. Crisp one-crown notes looked back at her. So it wasn't a robbery. But someone had obviously been in here. Why? Elsbeth scanned the room wildly. A few things were on the floor, but she didn't see anything missing. The glass jewellery cabinet looked intact. But where was Mum?

"Mum? Mum?" Elsbeth heard her voice leap out of her, higher than it should be. She ran into the kitchen, then upstairs. Empty. Then she remembered. Mum had said she was going to Lily's after lunch. Maybe she was still there? Her panic subsided a bit as she ran down the stairs to check the kitchen back door, where Mum would have hung her coat and handbag.

Elsbeth stood still. The coat and handbag were in the kitchen. She ran up to them. Mum's keys were in the coat pocket, and her purse was in the handbag. What did this mean? Elsbeth's mind had frozen.

"Um, Elsbeth?" Idris called. "You'd better come and have a look at this."

Elsbeth walked slowly back into the shop. Idris stood behind the counter, looking at the floor. A bunch of papers and cards that had been stacked in the drawers where Elsbeth's mum kept her important things were thrown about the place. "It looks like someone was searching for something," he said.

Elsbeth's gaze moved to the counter, and she let out a cry. Mum's hairpin. But not just any hairpin. This was the only hairpin that never fell out. The rainbow hairpin. It was studded with gems – one ruby, one emerald, one sapphire, one amethyst. Not real gems,

Mum joked. She just called them that. Elsbeth picked it up and closed her fist round it. Her mum's coat, bag, purse and the hairpin were here. Mum wasn't. Elsbeth's fingers dug into her fist even tighter.

Mum had been taken.

Chapter 8

Elsbeth's head was screaming at her and she tried to think. *Focus on the things you can control*, she heard Mum's voice say. But it didn't make sense. What would anyone want with Mum? Mum never really went anywhere – she hated leaving Lewesby. She had two friends: Lily, who she had lunch or tea with every time she went to her pawn shop, and another friend who ran the local café, whose husband had also died a long time ago. If someone had broken into the shop to steal stuff, they would have taken the money in the cash register – and besides, Elsbeth hadn't noticed anything else that was gone.

Mum didn't have enemies. Only Mr Lennox. And he would hardly come and kidnap Mum just because she hadn't paid the rent. Elsbeth grew cold. The only person who *did* have enemies was Elsbeth herself. Those HostTech guards. What if they had tracked her back to this Somewhere, and taken Mum instead?

"The guards in HostTech, Idris. You said they might be able to follow us. Into Nowhere."

Idris raised his shoulders helplessly. "I don't know. I don't know if they're advanced enough to do that. Why?"

"Don't you see?" snapped Elsbeth, and Idris's shoulders hunched round his ears. "They did come here. When we were in the attic – they must have figured out how we got there. They came looking for me and they took Mum instead!"

"We don't know that."

"What else could it be? We have to go back to HostTech, Idris! We have to find Mum!"

"I don't think that's a good idea," said Idris. He had gone very still, and his starry black eyes were watching her.

"I can't sit around here waiting for Mum to just … be delivered back. This is all my fault, Idris. I'll be careful – I'll stay hidden in HostTech and make sure nobody sees me."

"Elsbeth," said Idris slowly. "That's *really* not a good

idea. We can't go back there. You're supposed to be taking my advice. I know what I'm doing."

"Oh, and I don't?"

"Not really, no."

Elsbeth's eyes started to sting. "It's not your mum that's gone missing, Idris." As soon as she said it, she knew it was a mistake. Idris's mums hadn't gone missing. They were both dead.

He winced, as if Elsbeth had thrown sand in his face.

But before she could apologise, Idris exploded. "Elsbeth, don't you see? You can't '*stay hidden*'. You stick out like a sore thumb when you go to the other Somewheres! Everyone knows about you! You think you're doing all this stuff in secret: well, you're not. There are black-market traders crawling all over the Somewheres and when someone comes on the scene they know about it. We heard that there was a new Transporter all the way over the other side of Nowhere. I heard my grandmother talking about it, so I decided to come and check you out myself."

Elsbeth stared at Idris wildly. She felt everything around her going quiet. Everyone knew about her? The image of Mr Persimmon and his moustache loomed up before her. Was that what he was – a black-market trader from another Somewhere? And she had just been happily selling him the things she'd taken without asking any questions. How could she have been so stupid?

"Whenever someone goes in and out of openings, it creates a ripple effect," said Idris. "You've been travelling so much everyone has felt it. And you've been doing it from a new Sphere too. There have never been any travellers here before. So you got noticed pretty fast. But there's no way you can just go world-hopping now if someone has come and taken your mum. These people are dangerous, Elsbeth. We can't do this by ourselves."

"So this whole time … you were spying on me? You lied to me?" Elsbeth stared at Idris, tears in her eyes. Her cheeks felt cold, as if she had stepped out in the snow.

"I – not exactly. I – well, yes." The anger drained away from him and Idris looked like himself again. He hung his head. "I'm sorry. Really. I—"

Idris broke off. He stared at the street behind her. "Elsbeth."

The storm was back. Wind came whirling up the street and tables flew into shopfronts. Shrieks came from outside. Elsbeth didn't turn round. She could only think about Mum. She thought she'd been so clever. Sneaking off to other Somewheres. And all the time people had been watching her. Mr Persimmon, and now Idris, whose life she had saved. Who she had trusted. She might as well have been sounding a huge alarm bell like the metal plates had in HostTech: UNKNOWN. The shop door rattled as if it were being shaken angrily. And now Mum was gone and it was all her fault. Elsbeth clenched her fists and felt something burning inside her. Something rising.

"Elsbeth! Look behind you!" The storm was raging louder and Idris had to shout to make himself heard. Elsbeth swung round. Tables and chairs were being hurled through the street. It looked like a hurricane. But it was hard to focus on what was outside. Something was in the way. A shimmering wall.

It was an opening. And Elsbeth was standing right in front of it.

But it hadn't been there before. There had never been an opening in the shop before.

The ground began to shake.

"Elsbeth, you have to close it. Don't you see what's happening?" Idris cried.

Elsbeth panicked. "I can't close it! I don't know how!"

The shop was shaking so much now that pots were falling off the shelves and smashing on the floor. The glass cabinets rattled as if they were going to explode.

Idris stepped forward and took her hand. "Close your eyes and count to ten," he said. "You have to calm down." He started counting himself. "One, two, three…"

Elsbeth joined him, her voice shaking. "Four, five." But she couldn't close her eyes. What might happen next? She could hear shouting in the streets. What had she done?

Next to her Idris held out his hand to the opening, as if he were keeping it at bay. "Eight, nine." His eyes were closed and he was very still. Elsbeth realised the ground had stopped shaking. Then she saw the shimmering opening get smaller. It moved towards Idris's outstretched palm, as if it were being sucked in.

And then it was gone.

Outside the howling wind had disappeared. They stood in the silence, the debris of the shop scattered around their feet. Elsbeth felt the feeling of power drain from her. It was like sitting down into an armchair after a long walk.

"Elsbeth." Idris's voice was almost a whisper. "You just created that opening. And you did it before, in HostTech. That's why the ground was shaking both times. It wasn't an earthquake. It was you."

Elsbeth stared at Idris, then out at the street. Their neighbour at the fishmonger's had emerged into the street and was squinting at the now sunny sky, scratching his head. Had she really caused all this destruction? How was that possible? At the same time she felt that Idris was right. It explained the strange sense she'd had in the cell in HostTech. It was a new energy – something inside her. And it scared her.

But she knew something else as well. "I might have created them, Idris," she said, "but you closed them."

Idris stared at her. "No."

"Yes," said Elsbeth. "Both times you took my hand. You did it that time in the car park when you thought it was a real earthquake. And you did it just now too. You calmed me down, but you stopped it as well. I saw the opening flow into your palm. I didn't do anything. It was all you."

Idris looked at her and Elsbeth saw her own emotions mirrored in him. Confusion and fear. "Didn't you know you could do that?"

Idris let out a laugh a bit like a bark. "Well, I've never had to. I never came across someone that could create their own openings."

"Is that not something people can do in your Somewhere?" she asked with a sense of dread. She'd only recently learned that she wasn't as weird as she thought she was – that somewhere, out there, were people like her. But maybe there weren't after all. "Isn't it normal?"

Idris let out a wild laugh. "Normal? No. But I have learned about it. Nobody has been able to do it for hundreds of years, but it was said an ancestor of mine could do it. My great-great-great grandmother or something."

"And what happened?"

"Well, it was illegal. And it caused a lot of chaos. Even travelling through the existing openings causes instability, particularly from Spheres that aren't used to it."

Elsbeth thought of the unusual summer storms recently. Had that been because of her? She'd been using existing openings to get into Nowhere, but if they'd never been used before in her Somewhere, maybe even that had made the weather wonky.

"Creating new openings leads to all kinds of chaos, they say," Idris said. "It's what led to the formation of the Council."

"The Council?"

"They're kind of like the police for the Spheres. They keep an eye on everyone and make sure nobody's out of line."

More people watching her, Elsbeth thought numbly. "Black-market traders, the Council, your grandmother, you. Is there anybody who doesn't want to follow me?" But as she said it she realised she wasn't angry at Idris anymore. He looked so small and sad.

Idris fixed his starry black eyes on her. "I owe you an apology, Elsbeth. I know that. But you don't know what my grandmother is like. For once in my life I did something right, finding you. I thought she'd be proud of me. And then you needed help and I forgot I was supposed to be watching you. It just felt like we were the same, you know?" Idris looked at Elsbeth, an appeal in his eyes.

Elsbeth knew she didn't have the heart to stay angry at him. "Do you promise you won't lie to me again?"

"I promise," said Idris.

"I'm sorry about earlier," Elsbeth almost whispered. "When I said it wasn't your mother that had gone missing."

Idris shrugged. "S'OK." He looked away, and Elsbeth knew not to say anything more.

They paused, then Elsbeth said, "So what do we do now?"

"I think we go to get help," said Idris slowly.

"From who?"

"Well, you might think this is mad. But I think we should go to my grandmother. Racine."

"Your grandmother?" Elsbeth frowned. "But you're scared of her."

"Sort of. I mean, yes. But she's an incredibly powerful trader. She knows all the black-market dealers. If anyone can help us find your mum, then she can. And you're not safe here. Whoever came and took your mum might come back for you too. And if they knew what you could do! Creating openings. That makes you valuable. And in danger."

"In danger?"

There was a knock at the door.

Elsbeth and Idris swung round. A shadow stood outside, and the sun in the sky was so strong now that it was hard at first to make out who it was. There was only an outline of a hat and a raincoat. The figure had something poking out from either side of its face. A moustache.

Mr Persimmon.

"We're closed!" Elsbeth called out before she had time to think.

"I see that," Mr Persimmon's voice came. "I wanted to see whether you were OK. That was quite a storm."

"Who is that?" hissed Idris.

"I think he's a black-market trader," Elsbeth whispered back. "I've been selling things to him. Things from the other Somewheres."

"Well, don't let him in then!"

"No." Elsbeth suddenly felt firm. "I'm going to see if he knows anything. About Mum."

"Are you mad?" Idris asked. "What have I just been saying to you?"

"It's just one person," said Elsbeth. "I've been dealing with him already. I know him – a bit. I can handle this, Idris." She walked forward as she spoke, leaving Idris no choice but to hang back.

"I'm not staying around for this," she heard him mutter. She looked over to check he had gone through the back into the kitchen, then opened the door for Mr Persimmon to step through. "I'm sorry, you had a customer?" he enquired, looking around for Idris.

"He left," said Elsbeth firmly.

Mr Persimmon took in the dishevelled state of the shop. One corner of his moustache was raised. "I see you survived the storm. Your shop, not quite so well."

He took in the chaos serenely, then nodded at one of the walls. "The witch's eye survived at least."

Elsbeth looked round. On the wall hung a small

round mirror, with glass that stuck out like a bubble. You could see everything in the shop reflected in it – the mirror seemed to gaze around the room and absorb everything inside itself. As if you didn't really exist in the real world, but only inside the bubble. Elsbeth saw herself in it, small and doll-like.

"That's a butler's mirror," Elsbeth said. "It was used in dining halls so the butler could see what was going on without having to walk around the room. It's eighteenth century."

"Where I come from," said Mr Persimmon conversationally, "we call it a witch's eye, because it can look all the way around the room. People would hang it by the doorway to repel evil forces. It sees everything, you know."

Elsbeth frowned. Mr Persimmon seemed to be inviting her to ask where he was from, and she didn't want to go down that path. He probably wouldn't even tell her the truth anyway.

"Quite a storm, wasn't it?" he remarked.

But Elsbeth was in no mood to talk about the weather. "Have you seen my mother?" she asked.

"Your mother?" Both sides of the moustache were now raised. "I don't believe I have had the pleasure."

Elsbeth narrowed her eyes. When customers came

into the shop and wanted to haggle over an item, it was easy to get an idea of whether they were chancing it or would be willing to pay more. You could usually tell when someone was lying about what they could afford. It was an excellent way to get insight into people. Now, looking at Mr Persimmon, Elsbeth felt he was telling the truth. That, or he was an excellent liar. She reminded herself that he was probably a black-market trader; he had to be used to haggling in dangerous situations and remaining calm. But she had an instinct about it. She was willing to bet that Mr Persimmon didn't know where Mum was. But he might know something.

"She's missing. Her coat and handbag are here, but she's not." Elsbeth wasn't sure why she was telling this man, who she had met only the previous day, about her mum. But she was desperate. He might know something Idris didn't.

Mr Persimmon cleared his throat. "Should you not make inquiries to the local authorities here? The police?"

But Elsbeth shook her head. What would the police do? They could hardly go to other Somewheres to find Mum. They'd take Elsbeth away – she didn't have any relatives. Put her in a foster home. Then Mr Lennox would take over the shop because the rent wasn't paid.

No, Elsbeth was going to have to solve this by herself.

She thought about the HostTech guards. Idris had said she couldn't go after them. But maybe Mr Persimmon knew something about them.

"Someone … might have followed me," she said.

"Followed you? From where?"

"I was … I was in HostTech. I got arrested, but I escaped." There. She had said it. It was out in the open now, that they were talking about other Somewheres. Elsbeth met Mr Persimmon's eyes, and in that moment understanding passed between them.

Mr Persimmon stood straighter. "Then it's not safe for you here," he said in an altered tone. So she was right. He was a black-market trader.

"I should go after her," said Elsbeth.

"No, you absolutely should not. I can help you. But you need to come with me. Right now. Go and gather your things. I'll wait here."

"But—"

"But nothing. If somebody came for your mother, they will come for you too. I know people who can protect you. You have to trust me, Elsbeth."

It was the second time someone she'd only just met had asked her to trust them. Elsbeth knew she would have to discuss this with Idris.

But before she could say anything, the shop door swung open. Despite the CLOSED sign, this new arrival hadn't bothered to knock. Elsbeth could see why. It was Mr Lennox.

He strode in and looked around critically. "Just checking up on my properties after that storm. This place looks even more like junk now," he remarked. "I don't see how you're going to come up with the rent by the end of the week. The Lunden tourists are fleeing this place like rats from a sinking ship. Said that summer hurricanes aren't what they signed up for."

Elsbeth's heart sank. So the storms she was causing were affecting other businesses too. The whole town depended on those tourists.

"We told you we'll have it by the end of the week and we will." Elsbeth tried to sound firm.

"I'll believe that when I see it," Mr Lennox said. Elsbeth wondered if he'd be more pleased to be able to evict them than have his money.

"Still, just one more week after that and then the September rent is due too," he smiled.

"W-what?" Elsbeth stammered.

"Usually the rent is paid two weeks in advance. I allowed your mother an extension for August. But those were special circumstances. September rent is due next week. And the price has gone up again. Or didn't she mention that to you?"

Elsbeth stared at him.

"Where is your mother anyway?" asked Mr Lennox. "Not here by yourself, are you?"

Elsbeth felt panicked. Was he going to turn her over to the police after all this? But then Mr Persimmon, who had hung back while Mr Lennox spoke to her, stepped forward.

"Far from it," he said. "My niece and I are having dinner with my sister this evening, as it happens."

Elsbeth stared at Mr Persimmon.

"Your niece?" said Mr Lennox.

"Yes," said Mr Persimmon. "This is my sister's daughter. I've come to visit and get a little sea air."

Elsbeth tried not to laugh.

But Mr Lennox didn't look convinced. "First I've heard of Mrs Tawney having a brother," he said suspiciously. "I thought she had no family at all."

"I suppose it does make it easier to push people around when you think they don't have anyone to turn to," observed Mr Persimmon.

"I beg your pardon?" said Mr Lennox.

"Interesting thing about rent increases," said Mr Persimmon. "The law states it can't be done more than every two years without a very good reason. And tenants are supposed to be given three months' written notice. But you'd know all about that, of course, being the professional landlord that you are."

Elsbeth looked at Mr Lennox. His face had gone purple, and his breathing was so heavy that the tassels on the floor lamps were swaying gently. Then, to Elsbeth's complete surprise, he went to the door. "Evening," he muttered to Elsbeth, and without even the faintest threat about being back for the rent again – which, in Elsbeth's experience, was a first – he left.

Elsbeth stared at the door, trying to take in what had just happened. Mr Persimmon had lied to protect her. And he was offering to help her to find Mum. She looked at him, and for the first time, his moustache didn't look sinister. "You should go and get your things," he said.

But Elsbeth still wasn't sure. She stalled for time. "I'll go upstairs. I'll be back soon," she said uncertainly.

"Be quick," said Mr Persimmon. "This has gone on long enough. I can help you find your mother. But your own life could be in danger, Elsbeth."

Elsbeth went through the back door and past the kitchen, then stifled a yelp as Idris sprang out in front of her. His finger was pressed to his lips, telling her to be silent, but his eyes were wide. And frightened.

Idris turned up the stairs and Elsbeth followed him. He paused on the landing and she led him into her bedroom and shut the door.

"Do you know who that was?" Idris's voice came out in a high-pitched squeak.

"His name is Norbert Persimmon. I told you he's some sort of black-market trader. He said he can help me, but only if I go with him. He said I'm in danger."

"No kidding," hissed Idris. "We both are. But he's the reason, Elsbeth. That Norton Permuddon, or whatever he *says* his name is. He's no black-market trader. He's from the Council. I would bet my last peposa on it."

Idris was pale and stood holding his arms together as if hugging himself. Elsbeth drew closer. She realised he was shaking. "The Council? Those police people you told me about?" She frowned. "But that doesn't make sense. He knows I've been going to other Somewheres. I've been selling him things from them. If he wanted to arrest me, why hasn't he done it already?"

"He was gathering evidence, obviously," said Idris. "Seeing just how evil and wicked a trader you are. Once he's got enough evidence, he'll lock you up and throw away the key."

Elsbeth shook her head. She could hardly believe it. Had she been so wrong about Mr Persimmon? Her gut had told her he wasn't lying about Mum. And he'd just helped her with Mr Lennox. But maybe he'd done that so Mr Lennox didn't call the police. So that he could take Elsbeth away himself. And yet. He didn't seem evil. Not underneath it all. Elsbeth trusted her instincts.

Idris grabbed her arm. "I see you thinking, Elsbeth. But you have to trust me. We are in serious danger. He wouldn't just arrest you; he'd arrest me too. They have all sorts of rules about what you can and can't do. Trading and travelling – it's all regulated by them. They hate Racine, but they can never pin her down. She never leaves our Sphere, so they can't get her. But they've arrested people that worked for her. I'm not supposed to be here, so far from home. I don't have a permit."

Elsbeth frowned. "Is it a criminal organisation, then, what your grandmother does?"

Idris stood straighter. "My family has always traded. We're the greatest trading family in the Spheres. But the Council have been introducing more and more rules, getting more power hungry. That's what Racine says. They want to put us out of business, and we have to resist them."

Elsbeth hesitated. Was she any better than Idris's grandmother herself? She'd obviously been breaking lots of rules. She'd stolen things from that little boy's house, Elsbeth remembered with shame. It was the first time she'd seen herself as a thief.

But it was clearly too late now. Mr Persimmon knew what she'd been doing. Idris was right. Elsbeth looked at Idris. Both he and Mr Persimmon had asked her to trust them. But she could only choose one of them to help her right now. It wasn't a difficult choice.

"OK," she said. "I'm coming with you."

"We don't have much time," said Idris, clearly pleased. "Grab whatever you need."

Elsbeth took a bag and went to her chest of drawers. Then she saw her kaleidoscope on the windowsill, and her heart froze again. Mum. Where was she? *Wherever you are, Mum, I'm going to find you,* she told herself. *I'll get you back.* She reached for the kaleidoscope.

"A kaleidoscope!" exclaimed Idris. "I didn't know you had those in your Sphere."

"Why wouldn't we?"

"Well, they look like the place between Spheres. That's why they were invented. To show us what it's like in there." He picked it up and peered in. "Funny," he said. "The ones in your Sphere must be different."

"What do you mean?"

"I don't see the point of a kaleidoscope without any

colours," said Idris.

What was he talking about? Elsbeth grabbed the kaleidoscope off him and stared into it. She turned the end of it. Where normally red colours would have rolled into green, purple and yellow, now there was nothing at the end of the kaleidoscope.

"It wasn't like this the last time I looked," said Elsbeth. But when was the last time she had looked? It could have been a month or a year. It had become part of the furniture in her room and wasn't something she noticed much any more.

Idris shrugged. "Maybe the pieces fell out?"

Elsbeth turned the kaleidoscope round in her hands. The wheel patterns were dull in the daylight, but it didn't seem to be broken or have any holes.

"Maybe a customer came in here? Got lost on the way to the bathroom?" suggested Idris.

The idea made Elsbeth shudder. That a stranger might have come into the house – where only she and Mum should be. And into her bedroom too. But the thought that they might have then somehow interfered with the kaleidoscope seemed too odd. "Who would want a few pieces of glass?" she asked. The funny feeling between her shoulder blades was back. But there wasn't time to think about it now.

"Elsbeth?" They both jumped as Mr Persimmon's voice floated up the staircase.

"Just coming!" she lied. Clutching her bag, she and Idris tiptoed out on to the landing then up the stairs to the attic. Now was not the time to create another opening and wreak havoc. Hopefully by the time Mr Persimmon realised she was gone it would be too late for him to follow her.

"Here we go," said Idris after they had crept up to the opening by the attic window. "Are you ready?"

Was she ready? Elsbeth was about to allow a boy she'd only just met to guide her through the kaleidoscope to a Somewhere far away from her own, to meet his grandmother who was being watched by the authorities, and who – whatever Idris said about it – was clearly a black-market trader, and dangerous. Home wasn't safe for her any more; she was under surveillance from the Council, and Mum was gone. So was she ready to go and find her?

Elsbeth clutched her bag tightly to her chest. Yes. She was.

Chapter 9

Elsbeth stood in Nowhere, staring at the colours in front of her. Her Somewhere. She tried to fix it in her mind. She was about to travel further than she'd ever gone before, to the other side of the kaleidoscope. Somewhere completely different. She hoped she'd be able to find her way back.

"Which way do we go?" she asked Idris. Her voice sounded muffled in Nowhere, like it was coming through cotton wool.

"We have to go through the Corridor." The way he said it, it sounded like it had a capital letter.

"What does that mean?"

Idris squinted at the colours of the kaleidoscope in front of them. "Further to the right," he said. Elsbeth did her best to move that way, the heaviness of Nowhere and the backpack making her feel like she had rocks tied to her feet. The green colour of what Elsbeth now knew was the HostTech series of Somewheres started to dominate the purple.

"There it is," said Idris. "We need to go through it."

Elsbeth squinted. She had never seen anything like a corridor in Nowhere before. But looking at the kaleidoscope she realised there seemed to be a gap between these two Somewheres. It seemed to lead right into the middle of the kaleidoscope, rather than going round its circumference, as she had always done.

"We need to get to the other side. That's where I'm from," said Idris. "Go on. You go first."

Tentatively, Elsbeth took a step forward into the narrow Corridor. She was sure they wouldn't fit – the space looked barely wide enough for a cat to pass through. But immediately there was a sucking feeling. The Corridor was moulding itself around her – and around Idris too – pushing them with intention as if it knew where they were going. She held on to him firmly – she didn't want them to get separated now. The Corridor was now close around them and she felt as if she couldn't breathe.

Then, after maybe a minute, the Corridor squeezed

them out the other side, and they were in Nowhere again. Elsbeth stared at the colours in the kaleidoscope. She had never seen these before. So this was what it looked like on the other side – a beautiful sky blue merged with a butterscotch yellow.

"This way," said Idris, walking along.

"Where will we come out?" asked Elsbeth. "In another attic like mine?"

Idris laughed. "Unlikely. My Sphere is on the other side of the kaleidoscope. That whole thing about Spheres close to each other being similar doesn't really apply. It's almost certainly not going to be an attic, wherever this opening takes us out. But remember, people know about trading and Transporting in my Sphere. It's no big deal even if we turn up in the middle of a playground or something."

Elsbeth imagined just being able to pop out of an opening and people thinking it was normal. Not having to hide what she could do. Was this who she was now? Was being able to go to the Somewheres that much a part of her identity? She realised it was. Not being able to go to the Somewheres would feel like having an arm cut off.

Idris stopped and squinted at the kaleidoscope. "Here we are."

The colours were still yellow and blue, but there was more blue than before. The different types of Sphere obviously mixed together in the same way as on her side of the kaleidoscope. Then Idris took her arm and they plunged through into a Somewhere that Elsbeth instantly knew was completely different.

At first, her vision was blurry. For a second it was like looking at the kaleidoscope. Splotches of magenta red, stripes of waspish yellow, stars of teal blue and zigzags of pistachio green seemed to dance in front of her. Then the colours took form and she realised she was looking at hundreds of people in bright robes, tiny cars beeping and large yak-like creatures with long horns twirled round their heads like lollipops, all pushing past each other on a wide road lined with palm trees. Everyone seemed busy – drivers were arguing, chickens were squawking, older boys and girls were rushing along carrying boxes scattering tunes into the air. Nobody seemed to have noticed two kids appear at the side of the road.

A wave of nausea came over Elsbeth. She leaned forward. She thought she was going to be sick. "Idris," she managed to croak.

"It passes," he said. "It's because you went so far in the kaleidoscope. Give it a second." He sat beside her calmly, a smile on his face.

"Why … why aren't you sick?" Elsbeth said, gasping as her stomach turned.

"This is my Sphere," he said. "I'm home."

Elsbeth looked at him a little shyly. He seemed bigger in his own Somewhere. All the Somewheres she'd visited before had been similar to home. The weather had been cold in all of them, and it was often raining. And they had all been by the sea. Elsbeth looked up and around. They definitely weren't anywhere near a coastline here. Instead they sat at the foot of what seemed to be a large walled city on a hill. They were just inside the wall, near a busy archway, and when Elsbeth craned her head to look beyond it there was nothing but sand as far as the eye could see. Little cars weaved their way in and out of the crowds, barely moving faster than the people. They looked almost like eggs, with room for only one person to fit inside. Elsbeth peered down, half expecting to see feet running along the ground inside the egg. But there were no wheels at all, and they made no sound as they went along. She pointed. "What are they?"

Idris glanced over. "Solar-powered."

A man hurried past and Elsbeth caught her breath. She could have sworn it was Adam, who had left the lace shop in Lewesby. She'd seen similar versions of people she knew in the other Somewheres before, but that had always seemed to make more sense as they felt like versions of her town too. But to see a familiar face here felt jarring. She wondered if this Adam also had a Gry, or if he had fallen in love with someone else here.

"Why is it so different here? What was that?"

"The Corridor is how you get from one side of the kaleidoscope to the other," said Idris. "It's like, instead of walking round the circle, you blast straight through the centre."

"The centre?" Elsbeth crinkled her nose thinking about it.

"Look," said Idris. "See that bicycle?" A rusty black bike leaned against a vendor's stall. "The outside of the wheel is where we stand in the place between. What you're calling Nowhere. We walk round the edges, seeing the colours change as we move. But it takes a really long time to walk round the edge of a huge circle. If you want to get somewhere fast, you go through the Corridor – that's like the spoke of the wheel – to the other side. That's here. My Sphere."

Elsbeth thought about this. "But why are the Somewheres near each other – I mean, next to each other on the wheel – so similar? This seems totally different."

"It's Spheres, not Somewheres," Idris corrected her. "The Spheres are all a different version of Earth, overlapping where space folds in on itself. The closer the fold, the more similar the Sphere is." He sounded like he was repeating something he'd learned at school.

"I thought space was infinite," said Elsbeth.

"Yes, that's what some lesser Spheres think," Idris said, and Elsbeth had an urge to throw sand at him. "But really it's like a blanket with lots of folds and creases in it."

That also made sense, Elsbeth supposed. If the Somewheres were folded in on each other, that would explain why she came out in a similar place to where she had gone in. Like her attic and Victoria's attic: those two Somewheres must be folded very close together. And going across the Corridor to this Somewhere meant that the fold was more layered, so the Somewheres were more different. Idris was still explaining, but Elsbeth couldn't focus on what he was saying any more. Another wave of nausea hit her and she lurched forward.

"You should eat something," said Idris. "It helps." He went to a stall by the side of the road. A man with a long moustache handed over two packages in exchange for some coins. Idris returned, and unwrapped what looked like two pastries.

"I've missed these! Peposas!" he said, taking a big bite of the pastry, juice running down his chin.

Elsbeth thought they looked similar to the potato and cheese pastries Mum made at home. But when she took a cautious nibble she found her mouth burning with hot, spicy vegetables that she couldn't identify.

She tried to suck cool air into her mouth to relieve the burning feeling, and pointed at one of the creatures on the other side of the road. It almost looked like a cat, but had huge oversized ears that were as large as its body.

"What's that?"

Idris looked. "Oh, a chamcha. You don't have those, of course. The animals are very different here."

As he said this, the chamcha took a few steps backwards and shook its tail as if readying itself for something, then bounded forward and flapped its ears to take off. It swooped over their heads and Elsbeth laughed in delight, forgetting about her nausea. The chamcha's ears were translucent against the bright sunlight and she saw little red veins in them, beating with life.

"Come on," said Idris. "It's a bit of a walk up the hill. We've come out right at the bottom, I'm afraid."

He set off and Elsbeth walked after him through the crowds. Small children ran between the legs of men and women wearing wide-legged pants and tunics in bold colours: yellows, reds, blues. Most of the men had elaborate moustaches that reminded Elsbeth of Mr Persimmon – or plaited beards decorated with beads. The women mostly had their hair cut in sharp bobs along their jawline, giving them a determined look. It was late afternoon and the sun was already glowing a darker shade of tiger orange, illuminating a haze of dust that seemed to float above everyone's heads. Elsbeth wondered if all the families were on their way home to dinner. But nobody seemed in a rush. All the shops were open and their doorways were as wide as the rooms behind them, making the street feel like one large market stall.

Elsbeth noticed people staring at her. She supposed she must look very different in her jeans and shirt. She wondered whether they would work out that she was from another Somewhere, if trading and Transporting were normal parts of life here.

Then the heat and her nausea became too much. "Idris," she said faintly.

He turned round.

"Maybe I should sit down," she said, and plopped down on the road. "I don't feel great, actually."

"You look rather pale. And you're sweating," he observed.

"So are you," said Elsbeth. "It's boiling. I'm not used to this."

"I'll sort this out," said Idris. He looked around the street. "Here we go." A cart being drawn by one of the strange yak-like creatures passed them, driven by a man with a long beard that was interlaced with red and orange beads. "Excuse me," said Idris to the man. He looked down, surprised. His nose and forearms were sunburned so badly it made Elsbeth wince. "My friend here isn't feeling well and we need to go up to the top of the hill. Any chance she could hop in the back?"

The man shrugged. "You might as well both get in. I'm going home for the day."

Idris climbed into the cart and extended his hand to Elsbeth. She clambered up shakily and lay back, her head on one of the sacks.

"Where to?" the man asked.

"To Racine's," said Idris.

"Racine's, eh?" The man looked over his shoulder at them as if he hadn't seen them properly the first time.

"What do you want with her?"

"I'm her grandson," said Idris, a tinge of annoyance in his voice.

"You're pulling my leg," said the man. "I never heard of Racine having a grandson."

Idris let out a theatrical sigh. "You see how it is here," he said to Elsbeth. "It's like I don't exist."

Elsbeth frowned. "Does everyone know who she is then?"

The man swung round again. "Not from these parts, are you?"

"She's a Transporter," said Idris in a way that seemed to be meant to put an end to the conversation.

It didn't quite work. The man's eyes widened. "Is that so? A Transporter in my cart? Well, you're very welcome. Help yourself to an apple, why don't you?" He gestured to one of the sacks and Elsbeth reached out for one. Idris put out his hand too but the man shot him a frown. "You a Transporter too then?"

"I'm learning," said Idris through his teeth.

"Learning, eh? I thought folks were born with it, so to speak."

"Not necessarily," snapped Idris.

The man seemed to grasp that the conversation was over. The cart turned into a huge archway that led them up into another section of the walled city. Elsbeth lay back and stared up at the white stones above her head as they passed under it. The feeling between her shoulder blades was back and she frowned. "Idris," she whispered, so that the driver couldn't hear. "He couldn't have followed us here, could he? Mr Persimmon?"

"We'd know if he had," muttered Idris.

Not exactly reassuring, thought Elsbeth.

The cart rumbled up the busy street lined with houses and shops all made from the same white stone. Progress got slower the further they went. The problem wasn't the steepness, but all the people – and, as they got higher, the yaks. At least Elsbeth thought they were yaks, though they didn't have any hair. They were purple, with horns that spiralled out from their heads like snail shells. People were constantly dodging to one side to avoid getting speared. "What are those called?" she asked Idris.

He gave them a distracted glance. "Hyrelas."

The houses had been getting grander as they went up the hill, starting out as bungalows at the bottom and moving into buildings two, four and now eight storeys high.

Then all of a sudden the houses on one side of the narrow street stopped, and they drove into a beautiful vista, right at the top of the hill. The air seemed cooler up here – or maybe it was because the sun was setting – but Elsbeth realised she felt a lot better.

She could see the walled city spread out beneath them, the desert beyond it and, to Elsbeth's surprise, mountains at the horizon with snow capping their tips. The cart stopped and Elsbeth turned round. They were outside a huge stone courtyard in front of what looked like a palace, with large windows looking out on to the city.

"Racine's," the driver said simply.

Elsbeth stared at the great stone building. "Are you a prince or something?" she said to Idris.

He snorted. "Hardly."

Elsbeth stood up and the man surprised her by hopping down and offering his hand. "You're very welcome," he said. "Shall I ring the door for you?"

"I told you, I live here," said Idris.

The driver hadn't offered him help getting down so Elsbeth gave him her arm herself.

The bearded man drove off and she and Idris walked across the open courtyard, past a fountain arranged in a circle on the floor with jets of water that shot up unexpectedly from the ground. Elsbeth jumped aside as one sprayed her. They came to a tall wooden double door where Idris produced a key. The door creaked open – it was three times as high as their heads – and they walked into a huge dark hallway. A staircase marched up the middle of the room then parted and went to the left and right. The walls were made of a thick stone that radiated coolness. Elsbeth looked down at the floor – a beautiful mosaic with interlocking wheels was patterned on it. It felt familiar.

"That ballerina. From HostTech," Idris said in an undertone. "Do you still have it?"

Elsbeth felt in her pocket in surprise. She had forgotten it was there. She took it out. It was stiff. Elsbeth pushed its arms cautiously, but they barely moved. She couldn't imagine it dancing so beautifully here.

"Give it to me," said Idris.

Elsbeth frowned. "Why do you want it?" And why did he seem so nervous?

"It's always good to bring something back, when you see Racine."

Elsbeth had never had any other family except for Mum. She had always been jealous of friends that went to see their grandparents at the weekend and came back with stories of how much cake they'd eaten, and how late they'd stayed up at night. She'd always had the idea that grandparents were a luxury: people who would love you and spoil you and never get cross with you. She could tell that Idris's grandmother was something completely different.

"Are we going to go and see her right now?" She was slightly worried at the prospect.

Just then a young man appeared from behind the staircase, padding so lightly on the stone that Elsbeth couldn't say how long he had been there. He looked impossibly neat, and was wearing a tailored linen suit in a soft blue colour. *In this heat*, she thought. He stared down a long nose at them. "You're expected in the Round Room," he said formally to Idris, as if he were a visiting guest. He glanced in Elsbeth's direction but didn't make eye contact with her. "You and your friend."

"Expected? How does she know I'm here?" Idris asked.

The neat man gave Idris a sort of pitying look, before turning and heading up the staircase, clearly expecting them to follow. "Her people obviously saw us coming up the hill," Idris said under his breath.

The butler, if that was what he was, opened a door at the end of a corridor and they emerged into a wide, perfectly circular room filled with sunlight. A statuesque woman stood in the centre, a cup of tea and a saucer in her hands.

Elsbeth looked at her, and then could barely look away.

Her hair was black and cut close to her chin with a thick fringe high above her eyebrows like the frame of a painting. She had a long nose – almost too long, but the oval shape of her eyes seemed to put it perfectly into proportion. They were the same as Idris's – as dark as the night sky, with specks of white like stars.

"Idris! How nice of you to pay us a visit. And so soon!" The woman's voice tinkled as if every phrase were part of a song. Behind her, huge windows framed the city beneath them in its haze of dust and smog. "And you have brought someone with you." She spoke to Idris but her eyes were fixed on Elsbeth, looking her up and down in a deliberate manner, as she brought the cup of tea to her lips.

Elsbeth stared at Racine's long, perfectly manicured fingers. They were covered with gold rings and precious stones. The gold was of the highest carat, she saw at a glance, and the stones all looked real. Some she had never come across before – one was pink with a green hue shimmering around it. Racine wore a plain black dress and black shoes, but Elsbeth could see that the material of both was of very good quality. She became very aware that her fingernails were dirty and hid them behind her back.

Then her gaze fell on the long black chain hanging round Racine's neck. It looked like a firestone. It changed colour in the setting sunlight streaming in from the windows as Racine tilted towards them. It was the most beautiful thing Elsbeth had ever seen.

"This is my friend, Elsbeth," muttered Idris.

"Your friend?" laughed Racine. "But, Idris, you don't have any friends."

Idris stared at the floor and Elsbeth avoided looking at him.

"I'm only joking, dear boy. My, how seriously you take things." Racine smiled. "To what do I owe the pleasure of your company, back here so soon?" Elsbeth was quite sure that Racine was unhappy that it hadn't been longer.

Idris hastily held out the ballerina. "I brought this back. From HostTech."

Elsbeth managed to suppress a murmur of surprise at Idris's lie. Racine took the statue and peered at it. Sometimes objects from other Somewheres seemed more exotic out of their own world, but Elsbeth had to admit this wasn't the case here. The ballerina looked dull and seemed to have lost its sheen now that it wasn't in its own Somewhere. Elsbeth was sure Racine was thinking the same thing, as she looked up and smiled politely at her grandson. "Do you mean you Transported it?"

"I … yes. I did," said Idris, and Elsbeth flinched.

Racine looked sideways at Elsbeth, and Elsbeth had a sudden feeling as their eyes met. Racine knew. She didn't believe Idris for a second.

Then – and Elsbeth was certain she hadn't imagined it this time – the ballerina turned its head and stared straight at her. Elsbeth let out a squawk.

Racine simply looked down at the ballerina and turned its head back to face forward. Then she smiled her warm smile again. "Why don't we all sit down?"

They settled down into the plump sofas and Elsbeth had a sinking feeling not dissimilar to being sucked through the Corridor. She struggled to sit upright and regain control of the situation, but it was hopeless. She and Idris both sat with their chins almost level with their knees while Racine perched, straight-backed, on an intricately carved hardwood chair opposite them. Elsbeth found herself staring longingly at Racine's tea.

Racine saw her look. "What terrible manners I have. You must be parched. Idris, fetch our guest a glass of water."

Idris started to negotiate with the sofa.

"I can get it," said Elsbeth.

"No," said Racine immediately. Then she smiled at Elsbeth. "You are the guest."

Idris got up and returned with two glasses of water. Elsbeth gulped the cool liquid down as fast as seemed polite.

"Our family has always been proud of our heritage, Elsbeth." Racine smiled. "We run a vast operation here – from this very house – that trades goods across the Spheres. Transporters are trained from an early age – like Idris here, once it is clear they have the ability to travel. Although –" and here she sipped her tea disapprovingly – "it is rare for someone to show no aptitude whatsoever for Transportation at my grandson's age, even though they can pass through the Spheres themselves." She regarded Idris over the teacup. "He has been a great disappointment."

Idris seemed to sink further into the cushions.

"And where are you from, my dear?" Racine asked.

"I … I don't know what it's called." Elsbeth looked at Idris for help.

"It doesn't have a name," said Idris. "It's a Sphere Between. It's between the HostNat and the HostTech series."

"Ah," said Racine. "I confess I am not familiar with it. But I imagine it is a quiet place."

"Yes," said Elsbeth. "How did you know?"

"Spheres Between always are. They are not subject to any particular forces. They are like the backwaters of the kaleidoscope."

Elsbeth remembered that Idris had said that about quiet Spheres too. But she didn't like hearing her home described as a backwater. "It's actually very beautiful. We get a lot of tourists."

"I'm sure you do," said Racine. "I would love to hear more. But I don't think that's why you're here, is it?" She sipped her tea, and Elsbeth felt Racine's eyes fixed on her, watchful.

"It's my mum," Elsbeth blurted out. "She's gone missing."

Racine's hand stopped still, her teacup suspended in the air. Everything went quiet. "My dear girl," she breathed. "I'm so sorry to hear that."

Elsbeth felt she could handle anything except sympathy. Tears sprang to her eyes and she blinked them away furiously.

Idris jumped in. "We think she was taken by black-market traders. They were looking for Elsbeth." Racine looked at him calmly and didn't say anything. "We think," said Idris again, less certainly this time.

Elsbeth had managed to stop the tears spilling out. What was it about Racine that made Idris so jumpy, she wondered? He seemed very different around her.

"Why would these black-market traders have been looking for you, Elsbeth?" Racine asked.

"I Transport things," she said.

"I've never seen anything like it. She's amazing," said Idris.

Racine's gaze was still on Elsbeth. "Is that common, where you come from?"

"No," said Elsbeth. "Until I met Idris, I thought I was the only one."

"And then you discovered that you were normal. Relatively speaking." Racine smiled.

Elsbeth looked back. She wanted to tell Racine that she wasn't normal. She could create openings. Idris shuffled next to her on the sofa, and Elsbeth knew what he meant. He meant she shouldn't mention it to Racine.

"Tell me about your mother. How did her disappearance take place?" asked Racine.

Elsbeth told Racine everything she knew: the ransacked shop, the till full of cash, Mum's coat and handbag still inside the shop.

"And your father? What does he say to all this?"

"He died a long time ago," said Elsbeth. "I never knew him."

"I see," said Racine. "Well, I shall put our best people on this, Elsbeth, you can be sure of that. Any friend of Idris's is naturally a friend of mine. Benedict." Racine said the last word as if she were snapping her fingers, and the butler – though Elsbeth supposed he wasn't just a butler – materialised from a corner of the room and came forward.

"Tell Benedict everything he needs to know about your mother and he will take it from there," said Racine. "And then you both really must wash and dress for dinner. We have company. And, Elsbeth," she said, as she stood to leave. Elsbeth looked at her. "You are quite safe here. I will take care of you. You will be reunited with your mother." Racine smiled again. "Of that I have no doubt."

At the doorway she paused, her hand on the door handle, and turned back to Idris. "And, Idris. You finally brought something back from your travels. You've made me very proud."

Chapter 10

Elsbeth stared out through the tall glass windows. The Round room was at the front of the palace – from up here she could see that the fountain they'd passed earlier was also arranged like a wheel, with the jets of water following the patterns of spokes. Or the pattern of a kaleidoscope. Beneath them lay the city. Dusk was falling, and lights that looked like torches were starting to flare up along the winding pathways like rows of fireflies.

Benedict had just left, recording all the details about Mum in his notepad, and now Idris turned to her with a huge beam on his face. "She was proud of me!" He grinned. "I don't think she's ever said that I'd made her proud the whole time I've known her."

"Your whole life then," Elsbeth pointed out.

"Yes." Idris looked at her seriously for a minute. "I'm sorry I told her it was me that Transported the ballerina. But I was so worried she'd be angry with me. You don't know what she's like—"

"It's OK." Elsbeth cut him off. She realised she couldn't possibly tell him Racine didn't believe he could really Transport anything.

"Thank you," said Idris. Then, "Come on." He rolled himself off the sofa and stood up. "We should go upstairs. No offence, Elsbeth, but we might need to get a bit more dressed up for dinner."

"Dressed up – for dinner with your grandmother?"

"Dinners are a big thing with Racine," said Idris, leading her into a corridor. "There's always loads of people there, and they talk about business stuff. I don't normally get invited, actually. Usually I eat in the kitchen with the servants. Maybe this is a reward for being able to Transport," he said. He pushed a side door open and led Elsbeth up a rickety staircase that was far less grand than the marble one in the main hall.

Elsbeth frowned. She was sure that wasn't the reason. She looked down at her jeans and purple flannel shirt. It definitely wasn't an outfit for a formal dinner; Idris was right about that. "Where am I going to get clothes from?"

"You can borrow some of mine," Idris said. The staircase had taken them up at least five flights and Elsbeth felt sweat dripping off the end of her nose. They went down a corridor and Idris opened a door. "These are my rooms," he said.

Rooms? Elsbeth walked in to find herself looking at an apartment that was roughly the size of her and Mum's entire house. A sitting room with cosy if battered sofas had two corridors leading off it; Elsbeth followed Idris down one to a bedroom with a four-poster bed and a mattress almost as high as Elsbeth's chest. She wondered how Idris got into it each night.

"The bathroom's the other way," he said, gesturing, then he opened a wardrobe and began sorting through clothes. "I'll pick out a good colour for you."

Elsbeth went back to the sitting room and down the other corridor to a huge bathroom with cool sandstone tiles surrounding a sunken bath carved into the floor. Intricate wheel-like carved wooden windows looked out on to the street below.

She scrubbed her face with a black soap that smelled of honey. Idris appeared behind her. "These should fit you," he said, handing her a couple of things. "I'll change in my room."

Elsbeth took the clothes from Idris and felt the quality at once. Pure silk. She undressed and put on an embroidered green tunic over silken baggy yellow trousers. They had felt heavy as she held them but once they were on her body they felt as light as cobwebs, and cool as well. She looked at herself in the mirror. Her face was flushed with the heat but glowing, and the green of the tunic made her eyes sparkle. Elsbeth had never thought of herself as pretty, but this outfit was her best shot yet at feeling that she was. The person that gazed back at her looked poised and mature, with a certain knowing curve around the mouth that Elsbeth didn't recognise.

But that made it easier to face the dinner with Racine, she thought as they weaved back down the staircase, Idris dressed in a similar tunic but in red. She felt she had a uniform on.

Idris led her into a long dining hall lined with wooden panels. At the head of the table, flanked by two men and two women, sat Racine. The thrill of seeing her was not lessened the second time. Elsbeth felt a bead of sweat roll down her nose and rubbed it in embarrassment. Racine wore dark grey this time – a soft, silk material with a full-length skirt and structured shoulder pads. Her long neck made Elsbeth think of a swan. She still wore the firestone. When she spoke her voice had a touch of cinnamon in it.

"Please excuse my grandson," said Racine to the guests. "Keeping time is one of his many struggles in life."

Her guests smirked, and Elsbeth was seized with an urge to knock their wine glasses over. This was how it was for Idris here, she saw. He must have endured a thousand little comments like that from Racine, all chipping away at him over the years. It was amazing that he was normal at all.

She and Idris took their places at the other end of the table. There was a marked gap between them and the other guests, as if they were sitting at the children's table. Then an army of servants marched in and set down a dizzying array of silver dishes. "Please help yourselves," Racine purred at her guests.

Idris took the tops off the dishes at their end and they piled their plates high with cooked vegetables in tangerine and currant sauces, round flat breads shaped like wheels, and rice that looked as if it had been dyed different colours: violet, emerald, mocha.

New tastes began exploding in Elsbeth's mouth, all of them good. Some dishes were sweet, others salty.

She started experimenting with different rices. Then she realised that Racine and the guests were talking about the Council and pricked up her ears.

"They're getting desperate, I hear," said a woman dressed in a crisp white shirt with dark hair cropped close to her head and beautiful pearl earrings dangling to her shoulders. "But it's making them dangerous. I think there's a real possibility the Council might try to get back in here and interfere again."

One of the men, whose beard was divided into two plaits like pigtails, laughed. "Not possible. They know what side their bread is buttered. We keep things running smoothly and they don't interfere. That's always been the deal."

"You haven't come across the Council on your travels, I assume, Elsbeth?" asked Racine, her knife and fork delicately slicing the meat on her plate. To her guests she added, "Elsbeth is a visitor from a Sphere Between."

The guests' four heads swivelled in Elsbeth's direction, reminding her of the ballerina.

Elsbeth felt her cheeks burning. Then she realised it wasn't just her cheeks. She had just taken a bite of some lime-green vegetables in a fiery sauce and she gasped. Her mouth felt like it was on fire. "I … I…" Elsbeth's mouth was burning and she felt panicked. She gulped down a glass of water and it got even worse. She saw Idris nodding frantically at a bowl of yoghurt next to her, took a spoonful and exhaled.

Racine's face stayed smooth. She was waiting for an answer.

An image of Mr Persimmon and his moustache loomed before her. "N-no," she stammered. "But Idris has told me about them."

"Who?" the man with the plaits asked, chewing his food with his mouth open.

Idris rolled his eyes. Elsbeth stared down at her plate. Should she have lied? But she didn't want Racine to think she might have the Council after her. She'd never help her find Mum if she thought Elsbeth was going to be a danger to her. She would have to keep it quiet. She met Idris's eyes and saw he understood. Then she glanced up to the top of the table to see Racine's gaze on her, thoughtful, her wine glass suspended in the air.

The meal finished and Benedict came into the room, moving delicately like a cat to murmur something in Racine's ear. "What?" Racine said sharply. Everyone stopped talking and looked at her. Racine pushed back her chair. "We need to go down below," she said to the guests. "Right now. Elsbeth and Idris, you are dismissed. We will meet in my study after breakfast."

"What was that about?" whispered Elsbeth to Idris as they made their way out of the dining hall.

Idris shrugged. "There's always some drama with the business. She never tells me anything."

"And what did she mean, down below?" Elsbeth asked.

"There's a maze of corridors and rooms below the palace," said Idris. "It's where the traders come in and out from other Spheres. They'll have gone down there to sort out whatever the problem was, I suppose."

At the entrance to Idris's rooms, another servant stood waiting for them. "I'll show you to your room," she said to Elsbeth, ushering her through a doorway opposite Idris's. Elsbeth found herself in a huge bedroom with a four-poster bed that was scarcely less impressive than Idris's. Some pyjamas had been laid out for her and, feeling her legs and arms heavy, she put them on, letting her clothes drop to the floor, crawled into bed and passed out.

◆

Elsbeth woke with a jump. She had been dreaming that her mum was flying through the high street at home, her ears large like a chamcha's, with Mr

Persimmon in pursuit. Normally after a nightmare she felt happy relief upon waking and realising it had all been a dream. Not now. Instead she felt even worse. Mum really *was* missing. It wasn't safe for her to go home. And she was stuck here at the mercy of Racine.

Elsbeth stared up at the ceiling of her bed. It was like sleeping in a circus tent, the white netted folds hanging around her. Someone must have drawn the curtains while she was sleeping.

She stood up to find that someone had also washed and folded her clothes and set them on a chair next to her bed. It felt odd thinking that someone had been in the room. She dressed, then opened the shutters at her window and the light streamed in. Street cleaners were throwing buckets of water down the dusty paths and even at this hour the sun was beating down. It was finally quiet. The population of Racine's Sphere must not be morning people.

Then she stepped back with a little cry. A chamcha had fluttered down to land on the windowsill, folding its ears neatly along its back like wings. It turned its face to the sunlight and started to lick its paws, one of which had a large black spot on it like a birthmark.

"I don't suppose you'd like to be stroked?" Elsbeth asked it. The chamcha narrowed its eyes and growled in a firm manner that Elsbeth took to be a no. But it stayed on the windowsill with her companionably for a while.

She crossed the corridor to Idris's rooms, to find him waiting for her.

"Cardamom rolls!" he said happily, gesturing to a plate full of pastries that looked like they'd been tied in knots. Elsbeth could see the steam rising from them. Next to the plate stood a bowl of berries – not just the fruit that Elsbeth knew from home, but green, pink and yellow berries as well – and two pots. "Coffee and tea," said Idris. "I didn't know which you liked, so I ordered both."

"You – ordered breakfast? In your own house?" But Elsbeth didn't know why she was surprised. She'd seen enough of the way that Racine lived not to be. She looked at Idris. He looked small in this vast sitting room, and a little nervous.

"Was it strange growing up like this? I suppose you never knew anything else," she said.

Idris flinched. "I remember what it was like before. Before my mums died," he said softly. "I was only four but I remember it."

Elsbeth winced. She had put her foot in it again. "I'm sorry. What happened … if it's OK to ask?"

"They were both traders. Like you. Everyone in my family is, usually. But there was a long war with our neighbouring Sphere, and they were both killed. Racine made a truce with that Sphere, and now we trade with them as if it never happened."

"That must be hard," said Elsbeth.

"Well, I don't have to go there myself. Obviously. I wouldn't be of any use." Idris poured a large cup of coffee and offered it to Elsbeth.

"Tea for me," she said. "I don't know how you can drink that. It's so strong."

"I'm used to it," said Idris with a shrug. "And I'm sort of used to it here now." He bit into a cardamom roll and Elsbeth did the same. A sweet, buttery taste filled her mouth and she reached for another.

"And Racine lost her daughter," realised Elsbeth. "So it must have been hard for her too."

"You'd never know it if it was. We never say my mum's name. Racine wouldn't allow it. And she threw away all the pictures of her. There aren't any anywhere in the house. Except this one." Idris wiped his fingers on his trousers then reached into the pocket of his shirt and took out a worn-looking photograph.

He handed it to Elsbeth and she took it gently. Idris's two mums smiled out at her. One of them had curly hair, like her own mum, and her eyes suddenly stung. She blinked away the tears. It wasn't fair to Idris. Her mum hadn't died.

"You're thinking about your mum," said Idris softly, taking the photograph back from her.

"I'm sorry." Elsbeth sniffed and tried to pull herself together. "It's not the same, I know."

"We'll find her, Elsbeth. Racine is going to help you. I can tell she's taken a liking to you. And when Racine wants to get something done, it gets done. Come on." He stood up and brushed the crumbs from his lap. "We don't want to be late."

Elsbeth stuffed the last bit of the cardamom roll in her mouth and slugged back a final swig of tea, then followed Idris out of the room, back down the winding staircase and through the maze of corridors to Racine's study. She thought about what Idris had said. Racine had taken a liking to her? She frowned. She wondered what Racine was like with people she *didn't* like.

Idris knocked at the door then pushed it open, but Elsbeth realised immediately they had made a mistake. Racine's voice was raised. "I told her I won't negotiate!" she said in the sharpest tone Elsbeth had yet heard. She supposed that whatever had gone wrong last night after dinner hadn't been fixed. Benedict, his hands clasped calmly in front of him, was about to say something, when Racine swung round and stared at both of them. "What have I told you about barging in?" she hissed at Idris. Elsbeth backed away.

"I-I'm sorry, Racine," muttered Idris.

"We'll continue this later," Racine said to Benedict, who inclined his head to one side and withdrew without a word.

This time Racine didn't offer them a seat. She took short, abrupt steps to the great window and stood looking out. The snow on the mountains out on the horizon was glinting in the morning sun, but it was clear from the haze lying over the streets below that the freshness of the air was already fading. The city was waking up. "Forgive my sharpness," she said without turning round. "It seems we are having a little trouble with our neighbours again."

"Which ones?" muttered Idris.

"HostSchol," said Racine. Elsbeth couldn't tell if she'd picked up on the sarcasm in Idris's voice or not. "They are holding out on us and I fear we may need to do something drastic."

"Not something that would lead to another war?" Idris's voice quavered.

Elsbeth remembered what he'd said about his mums

having been killed in the last one. So that war had been with HostSchol, she thought.

"What does HostSchol stand for?" she asked.

"Hostile scholars," said Racine. "They control the knowledge in their society. Books are banned in their Sphere and the public is largely uneducated. Of course, that means the books are very valuable to traders – and for us."

Elsbeth frowned. "But should you be trading with them? If they're doing that to people?"

Racine raised an eyebrow. "You could look at it the other way – if we trade with them, we are introducing them to new ideas and keeping the lines of communication open. Our neighbours on the other side, BenSchol, do not have that option."

"BenSchol – so, libraries everywhere?" asked Elsbeth. And school at the weekends probably, she imagined.

"They are great exporters of knowledge, yes," said Racine.

"And do you trade with them?"

"We trade with everyone, my dear," said Racine. "It is not my job to fuss over how other Spheres are conducting themselves. It is my job to ensure that my people are safe and prosperous."

Elsbeth looked out at the city below. The beeping

of horns and chatter of local tradespeople floated up to where they were. Racine was obviously good at her job, she thought.

"Regarding your mother," said Racine.

Elsbeth's heart leaped. "Yes?"

"Our traders already have some lines of inquiry. I am confident that they will be successful."

Was that all? But Elsbeth remembered what Idris had said about Racine. When she wanted to get something done, it got done. She felt the tension in her jaw ease. Could it really be this simple? Racine would help her find Mum, then she and Mum could go home to the shop together, and life would be normal again?

"But before my traders pursue those lines of inquiry, there is one thing that you can do for me. In the meantime," said Racine.

So it wasn't that simple. Of course, thought Elsbeth. Racine was a trader. If she was going to help, she wanted something in return.

"I would be glad to help if I can," she said, trying to sound professional. Next to her Idris was watching them, like a spectator at a tennis match.

"Very well then," said Racine. "It concerns our neighbours in HostSchol. We have had an undercover spy in that Sphere for some years, who has worked her way up to their High Priesthood, as they call it. We held a meeting with her last night after dinner. She has managed to get access to a package of books from their inner sanctum: some of their most prized texts. As with all the books in HostSchol, there exists only one copy of each, so the value is virtually priceless. But there is a problem. She has been unable to Transport them herself. In fact, she lost one trying to do so last night. The amount of money that has lost us…" Racine closed her eyes as if in pain.

"So you want me to try?" asked Elsbeth. She heard Idris gasp next to her.

"You want Elsbeth to Transport some Old Texts?" he said. "Nobody has ever been able to do that before."

"That is not strictly true," said Racine. "Larsa was able to do it."

"But that set off the war," said Idris.

"Larsa?" Elsbeth asked.

"She was our greatest trader," said Idris. "But she died at the start of the last HostSchol war. Years ago, before I was born. Everyone still talks about her, though. They say she could see into the Spheres just by standing in the kaleidoscope."

"A word of advice, Idris, as you are new to this concept of 'friends'," said Racine, who had been watching him with increasingly pursed lips. "They don't need to know everything."

"Why wouldn't I be able to Transport the books, though?" Elsbeth asked. "Are they very heavy or something?"

Idris gave his bark of a laugh. "Only because they're weighed down by protections. HostSchol people can travel and trade as well – and they know how to protect their most precious things. It's very rare to be able to Transport a protected object. I guess the undercover spy can't do it."

"And you don't think I could either?" Elsbeth was conscious of Racine's eyes watching them intently. She wanted Racine to know what she could do. For some reason she wanted to impress her.

"I don't know," said Idris. "I suppose if anyone could, then it's you."

"That settles it then," said Racine with a smile.

"Can Idris come with me?" Elsbeth asked.

"Idris? He will be of no use whatsoever," said Racine, as if Idris wasn't in the room with them, standing right there. "He would slow you down and draw attention to you."

But Elsbeth knew she needed Idris. She could create openings and he could close them. If this was going to be dangerous, he could help her. "We've Transported things together before," she said to Racine. "We're a team." She looked at Idris and saw his big grin.

"As you wish," said Racine simply. "But we don't have much time." She consulted a watch that was attached to a sash round her waist, hanging down like a pendulum. "Our spy will be in place in less than half an hour."

"*Now?*" asked Elsbeth. But Racine was already walking through the door, clearly expecting Elsbeth and Idris to follow.

"What if I had said no?" Elsbeth whispered to Idris, as they followed Racine through narrow corridors that wound through the great house, which increasingly seemed like a maze.

"Nobody says no to Racine," he replied.

They came to a large stone archway and Racine ushered them through. "The Great Library," she said.

Elsbeth stared. They were in a huge circular room that seemed more like a ballroom than a library. Books lined the shelves to the ceiling and little winding staircases led to landings next to the books that were higher up. Elsbeth was surprised to see a chamcha curled up on one of the reading sofas, wing-like ears folded on its back, its whiskers twitching as it dreamed. She smiled to see the black spot on its front paw. It was the chamcha that had visited her windowsill.

Above them, a glass dome covered the ceiling. It had at least twenty spokes in it like a wheel. It looked like the kaleidoscope. She hadn't expected a room this beautiful, somehow. This was the kind of place Mum would love.

"There are books in here from across the Spheres," said Racine. "They are worth a great fortune – some are hundreds of years old."

Elsbeth gazed around. So that was why Racine had a room like this. It was just a store of wealth. And the books from HostSchol would make a nice addition to her collection.

A shadow emerged from behind one of the bookshelves. Benedict again. He did have a habit of appearing out of nowhere.

"We made the plan with our spy last night," Racine said crisply. "This library maps exactly on to the inner sanctum in HostSchol. Our spy will meet you there. She will give you the books, and you will come back here. If you are as talented as Idris says that you are, the whole thing should take only a few minutes."

She made it sound very simple, thought Elsbeth. As

if she were saying what the weather was going to be like that day. But the way that Racine and Benedict were staring so intently at her made her feel uneasy.

"What if they try to follow us?" asked Idris.

"Not possible," said Racine. "The opening in this library is under the strictest protections."

"So we're stealing these books then?" asked Elsbeth. "Not trading them?"

Idris stared at her. Racine's face was completely unmoved, but she looked at Elsbeth for a second too long before replying. Elsbeth wished she hadn't said anything.

"Our spy in HostSchol will be passing these books to you, and that is all you need to know. Payment for a previous trade has not been made, and it is necessary that we send a message. There is a new High Scholar in HostSchol who is apparently unaware that it is a bad idea – a very bad idea indeed – to cross me."

Racine had held Elsbeth's gaze during this speech and she carried on looking at her after she stopped. Elsbeth felt as if she were being pinned in place, forbidden to move, until Racine finally flicked her eyes towards Benedict and she could breathe again. The words *a very bad idea indeed* to cross Racine were ringing in her ears. She might have been wrong, but it had felt as if Racine were warning *her* as well.

"Do you insist on taking my grandson with you?" said Racine suddenly. "It is messy. I prefer things to be simple."

"I do," said Elsbeth. She turned to Idris. "If you want to come, that is?" If it was unsafe, she didn't want to put Idris in any danger. She had to go because of Mum. But he didn't.

Idris's eyes widened. "Of course I want to come."

Elsbeth turned back to Racine. "I think it's better if he's there too. Just in case." She wondered where her strength came from to disagree, but Racine only raised an eyebrow faintly. It was a small victory, but Elsbeth had won. Strangely she had the feeling that Racine was pleased. People obviously didn't stand up to her very often.

"The opening is here," said Benedict, ushering them to a spot right in the centre of the library. Elsbeth looked up at the domed ceiling, which was now directly above her head. The criss-crossed lines of the glass panes had surely been designed to look just like a kaleidoscope. Then she felt for the energy of the opening. Sure enough, it was there. Was this definitely an opening that was already there, and not one she had made? But the feeling was quite different. She could tell she was sensing something else, not creating it herself. Idris stood next to her and Racine watched them as the shimmer appeared in the air.

"You will find my mum once we're back?" she asked Racine anxiously. That was why she was doing this, after all.

Racine looked back at her. "I will," she said crisply. Elsbeth had that same feeling she'd had when she was talking to Mr Persimmon: Racine wasn't lying. She stepped into the opening, feeling stronger. This was going to help get Mum back.

Chapter 11

Elsbeth stood in Nowhere again. She was about to go into another hostile Somewhere. A place she had never been before. The last time they'd done this they'd ended up in prison. She felt scared. She was determined to do this for Racine, so that she would help her find Mum – but there was a deeper feeling inside her too. The thought of seeing more Somewheres gave her a yearning feeling. It was as if now she'd started, she couldn't stop. It was kind of exhilarating.

"We only need to take a tiny step to the left," said Idris. "This is it." The colours in front of them shifted almost imperceptibly. Elsbeth would never have been able to tell the difference. Another reason to be glad to have Idris with her.

“Thank you for coming with me,” she said. “You didn’t have to.”

“Are you kidding?” said Idris. “I wouldn’t let you down. Besides, this is a real adventure. I’ve never been to HostSchol before.”

“Never? But it’s right next door,” said Elsbeth.

“It’s too dangerous,” said Idris. He seemed to be about to say something else, but Elsbeth couldn’t tell what in the dark of Nowhere. The lights of the kaleidoscope flicking across his face made it hard to read. “We should go in,” he said. “We don’t want to be late.”

Elsbeth stepped forward and saw him hesitate. She had a moment of concern – had she been selfish, asking him to come with her? But then he followed her, and they were sucked into the opening.

They came out and for a second Elsbeth thought that it was Racine’s library again – but somehow here it was night-time. The room looked exactly the same, though. It was circular, with books going up the walls and little winding staircases all around them just like in the Great Library. But then Elsbeth looked up at the ceiling. There was no kaleidoscope pattern here. It was painted black, and dotted with gargoyles that stuck out from every side. Elsbeth squinted to make them out. They were all heads of birds, she realised, with long pointy beaks and eyes peering down at her. Then she looked at the books on the shelves and did a double take. Unlike the books in a normal library, with their different shapes and colours, these books all looked exactly the same. They each had black spines and nothing was written on them. "Why aren't they named?" murmured Elsbeth.

"Books are banned here, remember," said Idris. "I guess it's to keep them secret. Each book you see here is the only copy they have."

"But how do they know which book is which?"

Idris shrugged. Something fluttered down beside Elsbeth and she jumped, suppressing a squawk of surprise. This was no friendly chamcha. It was a large black bird with a long hooked beak and yellow eyes that stared at her suspiciously. It looked a little like a crow, but it was about twice as big as the ones Elsbeth knew from Lewesby. Had one of the gargoyles suddenly come to life? Elsbeth shuddered. This place was getting to her.

"A craw," murmured Idris. "It symbolises knowledge. It's their official bird."

"Where's Racine's spy?" whispered Elsbeth. The crow – craw, she corrected herself – stared at her and she felt uneasy. Could it understand what they were saying?

"I don't know," said Idris, whose eyes were also fixed upon the craw. "She's supposed to be here."

Just then a figure emerged from the shadows. It was hooded, and Elsbeth couldn't see the face inside. It beckoned them over to the side of the library, behind one of the winding staircases.

"Getting cool," it said in a low voice.

"I can lend you a jacket," Idris said a little too quickly.

A code, Elsbeth realised.

The figure removed its hood and Elsbeth recoiled to see a woman's face with a big black patch over one eye, like a pirate. But it wasn't the patch that was disturbing. An angry red wound continued along her cheek. It hadn't happened that long ago, Elsbeth thought.

"You must hurry," the spy hissed. "It's not safe." She reached into the folds of her cloak and brought out a parcel wrapped in black paper. The books.

Then she looked at Elsbeth and frowned. "I've seen you before," she said.

Elsbeth stared at her. "What? That's not possible." She searched the woman's face but it didn't look familiar at all. She was sure she had never seen her before. "What do you mean?"

"It's the hair," said the woman. "You have the same hair."

"She's not quite right in the head," murmured Idris. "We should go now."

But Elsbeth's eyes had widened. "She means Mum!" she cried, her voice too loud. "Mum and I have exactly the same hair!"

Suddenly, the craw let out a loud "cark!" Then "Cark, caark, caarrk!" it called, staring straight at the woman. It sounded like the alarm clock that Mum set in the mornings sometimes. The woman jumped and dropped the parcel.

Idris darted to pick it up, then handed it to Elsbeth. She shoved it in her backpack as he shouted, "Quick, back to the opening!"

But they were too late. Two more hooded figures were running from the other side of the library, straight towards them.

One of them grabbed the spy by the arms and pulled her back roughly.

"Have you seen my mum?" shouted Elsbeth at her. "Where is she?"

"Elsbeth, we have to run!" Idris dragged her back.

"Under!" the spy said. But then one of the HostScholars clamped his hand over her mouth. The other made straight for Elsbeth and Idris.

The two children tore towards the opening. But to Elsbeth's horror it seemed to be gone. It felt as if nothing was there at all. Had it somehow been locked, like the opening in Racine's library? But there was no time to think.

"Come on!" Idris tugged her sleeve and they raced over to one of the winding staircases, the hooded figure in hot pursuit. Idris went up first and grabbed books off the shelves as he climbed, throwing them down at the hooded figure's head. One landed and the figure fell back. But it started climbing up again, and Elsbeth knew it was only a matter of time before it caught up with them. Once they got to the top of the staircase, there was nowhere else to go. With two more turns they were at the top, the hooded figure only a few steps behind. Elsbeth had a moment of panic. What were they going to do?

"Jump!" shouted Idris. He sprang on to a ledge next to the staircase that jutted out near the ceiling, holding on to one of the gargolyes above his head for support. With no time to think, Elsbeth did the same, just managing to grab one of the crow-shaped stone handles herself. Then, swinging back towards the pillar of the staircase, Idris hit a button that Elsbeth hadn't seen before.

And the staircase disappeared.

With a cry the hooded figure tumbled to the floor below. Elsbeth winced, but the figure stood up straight away. It stared up at them silently, its face still not visible.

Elsbeth looked wildly at the pillar. Where had the staircase gone? Looking around, she saw that the stairs on all the other pillars were gone too. They were safe for now. Just holding on to gargoyles for support and trapped on a ledge.

"How did you know you could do that?" she asked Idris.

"It's the same in the Great Library at home," he said. "The stairs suck themselves into the pillar when you hit that button. I took a chance that it would be the same here."

Beneath them, more hooded figures had gathered. Elsbeth shuddered. What if one of them had a weapon? Their silence was unnerving, just like the black books with no words on them. Elsbeth thought of the scar on the spy's cheek. These people clearly had other ways of communicating.

"Elsbeth," murmured Idris, as the gathering beneath them grew to five, then ten hooded figures. "You know what we have to do."

Of course. Create an opening. "But where will we go back to?" she asked. "Won't we just fall through the air, if we come out in the same place in your library?"

"I'd worry about that later and get out of here first," said Idris.

Elsbeth nodded. She closed her eyes. She felt her body shaking. But this time it wasn't shaking with energy. It was with fear. And the fear was stopping her from concentrating. "I can't do it, Idris!"

Below them one of the hooded figures had stepped forward. "We suggest you give those books back to us," it rasped.

Elsbeth knew it was not a suggestion.

"If you do, you will not be harmed." The figure gazed up and Elsbeth saw the glint of its eyes, two red spots in the darkness. She thought she understood this Somewhere enough to know that it was definitely not telling the truth.

"Elsbeth," said Idris softly, "just close your eyes and forget about those things down there. Take deep breaths. I'll distract them."

"What will you give us for them?" he called down, to which there was a laugh from the hooded figures.

"Your lives," snarled the main one.

Just forget about them? Elsbeth thought. Just forget that

she was standing above a dozen or so mad hooded people from a hostile Somewhere that didn't let anybody read books, who obviously wanted to kill her and Idris, or maybe just disfigure them if they were lucky. She squeezed her eyes tight shut and tried to take deep breaths to summon the energy to create an opening, but it was impossible. All she could hear was her heart beating, as if it were going to break free before she did.

"We have money," Idris called down. "We could throw that in as well." To Elsbeth he whispered, "Your mum, Elsbeth. Think about her."

Mum. Mum, who she was here to help save. Had the spy really seen her? But no. Elsbeth shook herself. She couldn't think about that right now. Instead she conjured an image of Mum: her messy hairpins, her big woolly jumpers, her crosswords. She imagined Mum sitting in the shop, glancing up at her. *Create an opening, Elsbeth,* said Mum like it was a crossword clue. *Three letters.*

Elsbeth screwed her eyes tighter and felt the energy inside her. Suddenly she knew. She was stronger than those hooded figures down below her. And, just like that, the fear was gone.

The pages of the books on the tables below began to flutter. A breeze blew through the library. Then it wasn't just a breeze. The ground began to shake.

"What's going on?" snarled the hooded figure below them. Then the floor gave a huge jolt and he fell to one side. Cries came from the other figures as they lost their balance and books toppled down on them.

Idris took her hand. "You can do it, Elsbeth," he said.

Elsbeth knew she could. The shuddering got stronger. The gargoyle head next to her cracked and smashed to the floor of the library. She gripped on to hers tighter. It only had to hold a moment longer. Then the energy felt like it had come out of the top of her head and she opened her eyes to see a shimmer in front of them. But away from the ledge. To get into it they would have to step into thin air, or plummet to the ground below and into the hands of the hooded HostScholars.

"Come on, Elsbeth!" shouted Idris over the noise of the library books falling all around them. "We just have to jump!"

Elsbeth knew he was right. She leaned out, holding on to the gargoyle with just one hand. With the other she held tightly onto Idris's hand. Below her the eyes of the hooded figures glinted up at her greedily, expecting her to fall. She took a breath and felt her stomach lurch as she allowed herself to drop forward. She had the briefest moment of weightlessness – enough time to panic that it hadn't worked.

But then, to shocked cries from the HostScholars below, she felt the opening suck her in. It was over. They were in Nowhere.

Idris gasped for breath. He was still clutching her hand tightly. "That was a close one," he said. "Even scarier than that prison."

Elsbeth knew what he meant. They might not have been captured this time, but there was something way more sinister about the HostScholars. "What do you think will happen to your spy?" she whispered. Nothing good, she was sure of it. Idris's silence suggested that he thought the same thing.

"We need to go back to my Sphere," he said. "I need to close that opening as soon as possible."

Elsbeth shivered. "How does that work? Is there an earthquake in Racine's library right now?"

Idris shook his head. "Not yet. The instability your opening created will follow us to whichever new Sphere we go to. So we'll have to close the opening back in my Sphere, but we have to go through it first."

"But what about the opening we just left behind us? In HostSchol? Will the earthquake just keep on going there?" Elsbeth hadn't liked those hooded creatures, but she didn't like the idea of the whole city, with all the innocent people it surely had in it, getting crushed because of her.

But Idris shook his head. "No. We've taken the instability with us. Once we get back to my Sphere, it'll be like a tunnel that shouldn't be there, with the wind blowing through it. But after I mend the opening there, HostSchol will be fine."

Elsbeth nodded. They took a small step to the right. Then Elsbeth stopped. "Won't we come out into thin air, in the same place we were in HostSchol? We'll just fall to the ground!"

"I thought of that," said Idris. "We're coming through the opening from the other direction, which means it's next to the ledge. We can get back on that ledge if we just jump."

"Jump? From where?" said Elsbeth.

"From here. We just need to sort of run into the opening at speed and leap." Idris said this very calmly. His confidence made a completely mad plan feel more reasonable.

Elsbeth decided not to ask herself whether he was really as confident as he sounded. "I suppose we don't have a choice," she said.

"No point doing it half-heartedly, though. We really have to run and jump as fast as we can. Like you're doing the long jump at school or something."

Elsbeth nodded.

"On my count then," said Idris. "One, two … three!"

Elsbeth ran at the opening and pushed her foot as hard as she could into the squashy floor of Nowhere so that she sprang into the air. She hurtled into Idris's Somewhere and saw a bookcase coming at her at speed. She had aimed too low. The ledge was above her head, not under her feet. She shot her arms in the air and grabbed it with her fingertips. But she couldn't hold on for long. She already felt herself slipping. Then a hand caught her wrist. Elsbeth looked up, gasping for breath. Idris was crouched on the ledge, holding on to a stair next to him for support. "Hold on," he said. "This way." He began inching over to the staircase – still intact in this Sphere, the stone steps sticking out of the pillar reassuringly.

But Idris's grip on her wasn't steady, and his hand kept shaking. Elsbeth realised the ground was shaking too. Of course. The opening they had created was already making this Somewhere unstable. Just like when they'd escaped from the HostTech prison cell and arrived back in the underground car park in her Somewhere. Books began to rain down below them, just as they had in the HostSchol library.

Benedict raced up the staircase and Racine moved to the bottom of it, shielding herself from the falling books.

"Take my hand," called out Benedict above the noise of the ground shaking. Elsbeth heard a crack of lightning. The sky beyond the glass ceiling had gone dark, giving the Great Library the feel of the cloistered, gloomy blackness of HostSchol.

Feeling Idris's grip on her wrist tighten, Elsbeth leaned over to Benedict, who grabbed her other wrist. "Let her go," he commanded Idris, and Elsbeth swung through the air from one hand to another like a rag doll. Then she was on the stone staircase, safe with Benedict.

But Idris wasn't. He had begun inching back along the ledge.

"Idris! What are you doing?" Elsbeth cried out.

"The opening! I have to close it!" Idris shouted back. He crept back to where they'd landed and shut his eyes, and Elsbeth recognised that he was trying to summon the same calm that she had needed to create the opening in HostTech. But he wasn't as stable as she had been then – there were no gargoyles to hold on to for support. Instead he sat crouching on the ledge with both of his hands gripping on to it. With every shake of the ground it looked as though he would fall down to the floor below.

"You can do it, Idris!" she called over to him, but she couldn't tell if he could hear.

Then something unexpected happened. Racine had been staring up at the scene in silence, and now walked directly underneath Idris and stood gazing at him. Then she called out one clear, crisp word.

"Focus!"

It sounded like a command to Elsbeth, and she couldn't imagine that it would have made her feel calmer if Racine had said it to her. But Idris opened his eyes for a second, saw Racine, and after a moment of shock, shut them again. Elsbeth could see his body was less rigid. And within seconds the ground stopped shaking. Idris stretched his palm out slightly from the ledge and the shimmering opening dived towards it, just as it had in Elsbeth's shop.

It was gone.

Chapter 12

There was silence. Benedict was still next to Elsbeth on the staircase and Racine continued staring up at Idris. It was as though she were seeing him for the first time.

"Well done," she said to him. Elsbeth could tell that, this time, she meant it.

Idris seemed to shrink inside himself. He said nothing and began wriggling along the ledge to the staircase, where Benedict reached out to help him clamber on next to Elsbeth. Then he smiled up at her, and she saw tears in his eyes. They were tears of happiness, she realised. Because Racine had praised him. And for something he really had done himself, this time. She wondered if that had ever happened before.

They walked down the staircase to where Racine was standing. Books lay scattered around the floor and a couple of the reading lamps were cracked. The chamcha fluttered over to them and looked around disapprovingly, though its manner was very different from the craw in HostTech. Elsbeth didn't have the feeling it might peck her eyes out if it got annoyed.

"I will need to speak to my people," Racine said, looking at the sky above them. "They will be frightened."

The sun was back, but the thunder and lightning had only just died down. Elsbeth imagined that the people of Idris's Sphere weren't used to thunderstorms. They probably had no idea what was happening. She felt a twinge of nervousness again – she had caused this. But this time it was for a good reason. They had saved themselves from the HostScholars and she had done something for Racine. Something that would help her to find Mum. She reached inside her backpack.

"Here," she said, holding the books out to Racine.

Racine carefully undid the package and looked down at the black books. "Why did you appear from an opening up there? What went wrong?"

"They knew, somehow. The HostScholars. A craw alerted them and they came running to get us. They were chasing us and we managed to get up to the ledge." Elsbeth said this guiltily, wondering if this was strictly the truth. Had it actually been because she had raised her voice after the spy seemed to recognise her? Was it her fault that the spy had been captured?

"So the spy turned traitor," mused Racine.

"I'm not sure about that," said Elsbeth. "It looked like she'd been hurt recently. She was wearing an eyepatch."

"Even more evidence that she was a traitor. They tortured her, and she collapsed under pressure. Told them of our plan." Racine spoke crisply, without sympathy.

"But what will they do to her now?" Elsbeth said, remembering the way the HostScholars had grabbed the spy.

Racine held up a hand. "We will do what we can. But that's not important right now. I want to know what just happened here. If I am not mistaken, what I just witnessed was a newly created opening being closed. By my grandson himself. My question is, who created it?"

Elsbeth knew there was no hiding it.

"I did," she said.

Racine stared at her for a long time. "Do you know how you're doing it?" she asked softly.

"I – yes. I mean, I do now. At first it just happened when I got scared. Back at home, near my Some— my Sphere. Then we realised that Idris was closing the openings I had made, calming things down. He hadn't known either."

"So that's why you wanted Idris to go with you to HostSchol," said Racine slowly. "To help you in case things went wrong."

"Yes," said Elsbeth. "That and, well, we're a team now."

Idris smiled at her gratefully.

Racine turned to him. "All this time I thought you had no talents. It turned out I was just looking in entirely the wrong place for them."

Elsbeth winced at this but Idris beamed again. He really must not have received many compliments in his life if he thought that this was high praise. It was true, though. Idris undeniably had a talent. She supposed she did too.

As if Racine could hear Elsbeth's thoughts, she said, "I wonder if there are any two people across the kaleidoscope who possess the talents both for creating openings and for closing them. And who have been fortunate enough to find each other. Think of the things you could do together."

But Racine didn't seem pleased or excited. Her smooth forehead was creased and she looked past Elsbeth and Idris, as if addressing someone invisible.

"Will your traders go to find Mum now?" Elsbeth asked.

Racine glanced at her distractedly. "Of course. It was never a condition that you go to HostSchol. You could have refused."

No I couldn't, thought Elsbeth, but aloud she simply said, "Thank you."

"Before we make any plans," said Racine – and Elsbeth's heart sank – "I have to address my people. They will be scared, after that thunderstorm you called down upon us."

"I didn't call it down," said Elsbeth. "I didn't mean to do it. I'm sorry."

"Well, we need to make it right. You will both come with me in the open carriage. The two of you should go and change into something more suitable. Benedict, make the preparations. We will leave in half an hour."

Racine swept out of the room.

Idris scratched his head. "The open carriage! She's never taken me in that before. She obviously does think I'm special now."

She should have thought you were special anyway, because

you're her grandson, Elsbeth thought, but she didn't say it aloud. Idris looked so pleased. But the spy's words were still ringing in her ears. *I've seen you before,* she had said. And then, right before the hooded figures put a hand over her mouth and stopped her speaking, *Under.* Had she really been talking about Mum? And what did "Under" mean?

"What do you think that spy meant, when she said she'd seen me before?" she said to Idris as they hurried to their rooms to change.

"If she'd been tortured, she would say anything," said Idris. "She'd probably lost her mind. She was seeing things."

"But Mum and I do have the same hair. Exactly the same. And we do look similar. Everyone says it. It sounded like she had seen Mum," insisted Elsbeth.

"How, though?" reasoned Idris. "Your mum went missing way over on the other side of the kaleidoscope. The spy spends all her time here and in HostSchol."

"Under the palace!" said Elsbeth. "The spy said under! That could mean down below – you said last night the traders from other Spheres come in below the palace! We have to go down there and check it out!"

Idris crinkled his nose. "Look, Elsbeth, I think you're hoping that anything could be a clue to find your mum because you want to find her," he said. "And I'm sorry. I'm sure that Racine is going to help you. She does keep her word, you know. But not if we don't keep ours. And we promised we would go and meet her. Trust me, Elsbeth, you don't want to keep her waiting. We can think properly about what the spy meant later, after we've changed and gone out."

"What's wrong with what we have on now?" asked Elsbeth. Her long tunic felt like the smartest thing she'd ever worn.

Idris glanced down at her as they climbed the narrow staircase to his rooms. "I don't think you understand what a big deal going in Racine's open carriage is. It's huge. She only goes out in it twice a year – on her birthday, usually, and on the anniversary of us winning the HostSchol wars. Everyone comes out into the streets to see it, and she waves at the crowds, then talks to them in the main square."

Like the king in Lunden back in her own Somewhere, Elsbeth thought. Dressing for dinner, and now dressing for the carriage. Being with Racine seemed to involve a lot of thinking about your appearance. She realised that Racine had managed to dodge the question of finding Mum, while making Elsbeth feel guilty, as if the only right thing to do was address her people. Things were happening on Racine's terms, when *she* wanted them to. How could she make Racine feel the same urgency about finding Mum that she did? She had made up her mind about one thing, though – when they got back she was going to go and explore those rooms below the palace. She didn't care what Idris said about the spy losing her mind. If there was any chance she knew where Mum was, Elsbeth had to check it out.

When she got to her room, she found that someone had already laid out fresh clothes on her bed. They were made of pure silk, with embroidered patterns on the sleeves in a silvery thread that sparkled. Another kaleidoscope pattern. She went to the windowsill and picked up Mum's kaleidoscope, which she had left there to try to feel more at home. She held it up to her eye, but of course it was still empty. With a start, she realised that the chamcha that had been in the Great Library was back on her windowsill.

"Are you following me?" she asked it with a smile. The chamcha narrowed its eyes, which she took to be a shrug. "It's funny having a kaleidoscope with no colours in it," she confided to it. "This used to have them in, but they've disappeared. What would anyone want with a few bits of glass?"

The chamcha had been observing Elsbeth as

she spoke, and now it dropped off the windowsill so suddenly that she gasped and leaned over, worried that it had forgotten how to fly. But it was already lumbering upwards, its ears pushing oddly majestically against the air, until it disappeared over the rooftops of the small houses lower down. Elsbeth watched it go. Its legs were about half the length of the cats' at home. She supposed it didn't need to use them as much.

"Talking to a chamcha now about my problems," she murmured.

A crashing sound came from behind the houses and a man's voice shouted "Hey!" The chamcha reappeared, its ears beating with more purpose now. It had something in its mouth, Elsbeth realised. It landed back on the windowsill with a bump and dropped the object in front of her.

Elsbeth stared down at it. It was her kaleidoscope.

But it wasn't her kaleidoscope. That was in her hand. Elsbeth looked down at herself holding it, to be quite sure. This one looked exactly the same, though. It was cleaner, and less scuffed, but it had the same yellow colour with green criss-crosses decorating it. It had a little label hanging off it and Elsbeth looked closer. 2D. She wasn't sure what that meant, but it looked like a price tag. She lifted it to her eyes and looked through it. This one had its glass pieces in it – it was a normal kaleidoscope. She stared at the chamcha. "How did you know?" she breathed.

The chamcha turned its face to the sun, its work done, and began to lick its paw.

Elsbeth stared down at the two kaleidoscopes she was holding. There was no mistaking it – it was exactly the same design. Another version of the same thing. But Mum had given her the kaleidoscope as a present. Had she bought it from a black-market trader in Lunden maybe, without realising where it was from? But why would she? A kaleidoscope from another Somewhere would be far more expensive than a kaleidoscope made in Elsbeth's own Somewhere. Any black-market trader would know that. Kaleidoscopes weren't that hard to make. So how would this particular kaleidoscope, which was clearly a cheap trinket here in Idris's Somewhere, make it all the way across the Corridor to Elsbeth's Somewhere? And it had to have been years ago too, Elsbeth realised. Mum had given this to her when she was eight. It didn't make sense.

There was a knock at the door and she looked up to see Idris.

"Elsbeth? Is everything OK?" He looked at the two kaleidoscopes that Elsbeth was clutching, one in each hand. "You got another one?"

"Where did this come from?" Elsbeth said slowly.

"Those?" said Idris. "They're very common around here. They sell them at all the shops. They're for little kids usually."

"But this is exactly the same as my kaleidoscope!" Elsbeth cried. "Look!" She thrust both in front of Idris, who wrinkled up his nose and looked confused.

"Yes, you showed me this before. In your bedroom? At home?"

"But now there are two!" Elsbeth couldn't understand why Idris didn't think this was strange. She continued more slowly. "My kaleidoscope – the one that Mum gave me – comes from your Somewhere. How is that possible? Nobody in my Somewhere can travel. Where would she have found it?"

But before Idris could say anything, there was a knock at the door. "The carriage is waiting," came Benedict's voice.

The thought of getting in an open carriage with Racine and driving through streets full of people right now made Elsbeth feel sick. "I can't go," she hissed.

"Are you mad?" Idris said. "Racine will be furious. We need to keep her on our side. And like she said, we're the reason that she has to do this in the first place.

People will be scared – all because of us, because we created an opening."

That wasn't strictly true, thought Elsbeth, as she reluctantly allowed Benedict to hurry her and Idris along the corridors and back down a new staircase she hadn't seen before. They wouldn't have had to create an opening if Racine hadn't sent them to HostSchol to steal some books. But she still felt guilty, so when they emerged into the bright sunlight, the heat hitting her like a slap in the face, she allowed herself to be ushered into the huge silver carriage and sat opposite Racine. "Idris," she tried again. But he glared at her. "Later," he whispered.

Racine had changed, and now wore a long cream gown that dripped to her feet, and a thin cream scarf that she wore backwards round her neck, the ends falling down her back. The firestone glowed with a white light, matching her outfit. She nodded to Benedict, who sat in front of her holding the reins of the hyrelas, and they began to move. Elsbeth glanced around her mutely. Outwardly she was still but her thoughts were racing. How had the kaleidoscope that Mum had given her travelled all the way from this Somewhere to hers? Had the spy really seen Mum before? And when would she be able to get underground – to get away from Racine

– and find out more for herself?

The carriage rattled on through small winding streets. Racine sat upright, coolly waving at the people they passed.

Elsbeth could see the destruction the storm had caused, even though it had been brief. They moved past a market where fruit and vegetables had tumbled to the ground, some smashed wide open. Elsbeth felt a fresh wave of guilt to see people on their hands and knees by their ruined stalls, picking up what they could and muttering to each other. But they stood up respectfully as Racine's carriage passed by. One of the men handed them some fruit, and Elsbeth bit down on the purple berries to find they tasted of sherbet that tingled in her mouth. Another woman pressed some cardamom rolls on to them, which Racine accepted graciously. Elsbeth relished the sweet, buttery taste again. She felt starving, despite her worry about Mum. Perhaps creating openings was hungry work.

"Everything is OK," Racine assured various people asking her what had happened.

"What was that storm?" said one woman. "It wasn't natural, surely."

"Not the HostScholars causing trouble again, I hope?" asked one older man anxiously.

"Nothing like that, I assure you," Racine said.

Elsbeth was surprised to see how natural Racine was with the people, and how easy they seemed to find it to talk to her and ask questions. She couldn't imagine the king at home in Lunden ever being like that. Yet they respected her too. Elsbeth had the feeling that if they didn't show Racine enough respect then things would be very different. She was sure they wouldn't dare.

Then, when Racine was engaged in conversation with someone else, Elsbeth whispered to Idris, "How did the chamcha know?"

"Know what?"

"I was talking to it. About my kaleidoscope. And then it went and got another one from somewhere and brought it to me."

"It must have taken a shine to you," remarked Idris. "Chamchas never do anything I say."

"But I didn't tell it to do anything! How could I? It can't talk!"

Idris looked surprised. "No, but it can understand us, of course. Can't the animals in your Sphere understand you?"

"Idris," came Racine's voice, "don't slouch."

They both sat upright. The carriage was moving

into a great square now, paved with little white stones like a mosaic. Elsbeth saw the stones also formed the triangles of the kaleidoscope, just as the fountain outside Racine's palace had done. It was crowded with people.

The carriage stopped. "I will get out now and walk among the people," Racine announced. "You can both assist me." But the heavy heat of midday, the shock of the morning's events and the lurching of the carriage had taken its toll on Elsbeth and she suddenly felt faint.

"She looks very pale," said Idris.

Racine sighed. "Very well. I shall go myself. Benedict." Benedict hopped down from the front and gave her his hand to help her down. "Idris, get Elsbeth some sugar water from that stall over there. And take my parasol. I suppose she is unused to this heat."

Racine began to walk through the square, stopping to clasp hands and ask questions. It was clear that everyone admired her, which was no great surprise. She looked like a chess piece, her cream gown stiff and her black bob unmoving as she glided effortlessly around while Benedict stayed at her side, stopping people from overstaying their welcome.

Idris hopped down. "I'll be back in a minute," he said, nodding at a nearby stall. "You're probably dehydrated. You have to drink a lot when it's hotter than you're used to."

Elsbeth laid back in the carriage, feeling annoyed at herself. Now was not the time to be struggling because of the weather. She needed to be able to think. She just wished it were cooler. She gazed across the square.

And then her heart leaped in her throat.

At the other end of the square was a large white archway, standing by itself, as if it had once been attached to a wall that had long since been destroyed. Couples were posing under it to have their pictures taken.

When she and Idris arrived in this Somewhere, at the side of the road inside the city walls, she had had the strangest feeling she'd been here before in a dream. Of course, she hadn't. But now, looking at the archway in front of her, she realised she had seen this Somewhere before. She'd seen it every day of her life. In the picture of Mum and Dad in the shop behind the counter. Because *they* had been right here. Standing under the archway in the main square, smiling into the sun.

Idris reappeared, holding two sugar waters. "I've missed these," he said, holding one out to Elsbeth. Then he saw her face. "You look worse," he said anxiously.

"Maybe you should lie down."

"Idris!" Elsbeth cried. "My mum has been here before! To this Sphere!"

Idris frowned. "But I thought she couldn't travel."

"Of course she can't travel!" Didn't Idris see that this made no sense at all? "She has no idea about the Somewheres. She's … normal! She never even leaves Lewesby."

"So why do you think she's been here then?" asked Idris cautiously.

"There's a photo at home. And it shows her and Dad, right here. Right here, Idris!" Elsbeth wondered if she was going mad. Nothing made sense any more.

"OK, let's just think about it. It's OK, Elsbeth," said Idris. It was as if he were closing an opening she'd made. Elsbeth felt the same sense of calm come over her.

"Why did your mum not like to leave Lewesby?" Idris asked.

"She says it's her home."

"Born there, was she?"

"No. She came from Scotland originally. But then her family kicked her out because they didn't approve of my dad, and then he got sick and died, and she was pregnant with me and came to Lewesby. She always said that was enough adventure for one life, and she just wanted to live quietly."

"Hmm," said Idris. "Why didn't her family approve of your dad?"

"I don't know exactly," said Elsbeth. "Her family was rich and his wasn't. She always used to say they were from different worlds."

The double meaning of this phrase that Mum had always used, here in a different Sphere on the other side of the kaleidoscope, hit Elsbeth with force and she saw that Idris was thinking the same thing.

"Different … worlds?" he said.

They stared at each other.

Elsbeth shook her head. "No, no, no. It isn't possible." An image of Mum in the shop with her crossword flashed before her. Mum sitting with her tea, calm as always, never ruffled by anything. But what did she really know about Mum's life before Lewesby? Mum had never gone into much detail about her family. All Elsbeth knew was that they were very posh, and Dad hadn't been. Mum and Dad had met by the seaside; she knew that much. That was why Mum had wanted to move to Lewesby after he had died; the sea air reminded her of him. But she hardly knew anything else about their lives together. Except that they had travelled a lot, Mum said. They had been all over the world.

Or was it all over the *worlds*, plural?

What if Mum hadn't meant just her Somewhere? She and Dad had travelled here together. Elsbeth stared back at the archway. There was no mistaking it. It even had the same little pillars going up the sides of it, which she now realised were actually kaleidoscopes.

Everything started to make sense, even though everything had been turned upside down. So Mum could travel. And that explained why Elsbeth could. And now Mum was missing, and she had no idea why. Maybe she hadn't even gone missing at all – maybe she had just left Elsbeth and gone somewhere new. The thought was like a cold cloth on her chest. But Elsbeth knew one thing for sure now: she had no idea who her mother was at all.

Chapter 13

The sun beat down on them. Elsbeth sat sweating under the shade of the parasol, which felt barely any less scorching than the sun itself. Everything had changed. She didn't know what was real and what wasn't. Mum was a traveller, like her. Mum had been inside the kaleidoscope. How could she never have said anything? Why had she never told Elsbeth?

"Let's try to think," said Idris. "OK, so your mum can travel, like you can. That's not so unusual. It explains why you can, doesn't it? You didn't just get that ability from nowhere. So that kind of makes sense at least."

Idris spoke in a soothing voice. Elsbeth felt anything but calm. Too many thoughts were racing through her head. But she forced herself to sip her sugar water and listened to him.

"Supposing your mum *had* been here before," he continued. "What would that mean? How does it help us to find her?"

"We have to ask Racine," whispered Elsbeth. "Maybe she knew Mum. Maybe she met her all those years ago."

Idris frowned. "That seems unlikely. Why would they have met?"

Elsbeth looked over to where Racine was, still surrounded by a throng of people, still cool and calmly answering questions. She turned to make her way back to the carriage and caught Elsbeth looking at her. Elsbeth had the now familiar jolt of electricity when she found herself in Racine's eyeline. But she was tired of being scared of her. Racine had been putting her off from finding Mum ever since she got here, Elsbeth thought, making her go to dinner with people she didn't know, then putting her in danger in HostSchol, then making her feel guilty about it and now taking her for this weird open carriage ride in the sweltering heat. And Elsbeth kept putting up with it.

Racine was at the carriage now. Benedict helped her up and she sat down opposite Elsbeth and arranged her skirts. She looked as if she had just been reading a book, not walking around a square in the midday sun for half an hour.

"How are you feeling, my dear?" Racine's voice was cool. "You look better," she added. "You have quite a colour in your cheeks now."

"Racine, I need to talk to you," said Elsbeth.

"I had a lot of questions about who you were," continued Racine, as if Elsbeth hadn't said anything.

This threw Elsbeth. "About me?"

"I told them you were a great trader," said Racine. "And that they would no doubt be hearing a lot more about you."

Elsbeth frowned. She looked out at the crowds and realised that a number of curious glances were being thrown her way. Her cheeks flared up. Why had Racine taken her out here and let people see her? It was almost like she was showing her off or something. Like she was some prize pig.

"You *have* got a lot of colour," Racine said, then smiled out at the people and waved at them.

The carriage started moving again and Elsbeth took a deep breath. Her heart was beating fast. At least now that her face was already red it didn't matter if she embarrassed herself by asking Racine about Mum.

"The thing I wanted to ask you," she began.

Racine didn't turn round.

"Racine!" she said firmly. Racine turned to her with both eyebrows raised, and Elsbeth was conscious that Idris was staring at her.

"I wanted to ask you about my mum," she said.

"As I have told you, we have started our search," said Racine. "I've put our best traders on it – she will turn up soon. But there is much work to be done here – we have to repair the damage that your opening did." Racine was talking faster than usual.

But Elsbeth wasn't going to let herself get distracted – or feel guilty – again.

"The thing is," she said, raising her voice so that Racine couldn't pretend she hadn't heard, even though they were sitting opposite each other. "I think my mum has been to this Somewhere – to this Sphere – before. In fact, I know she has."

Racine stared at her. "What do you mean?"

"There's a picture in our shop. Of her and my dad. It's the only one she has of them together. Before he died. They were standing beneath a white archway in the sun, smiling. It's the archway I saw in the square just now. The exact same one. I know it is."

But Racine just smiled. "Is that your only evidence? I'm surprised at you, Elsbeth. You know that Spheres near each other are very similar. Sometimes it's impossible to tell where you are until you hear the history of the place. Why, that archway could be in any number of Spheres close to here."

Elsbeth's heart sank. Of course. Racine was right. Mum might have been somewhere similar, but that didn't mean she'd definitely been to this Sphere. "So I suppose you don't know her then," she said sadly. "Penelope Tawney? I thought maybe you might have met her."

"A Penelope Tawney, you said?" asked Racine. "I can assure you I have never met a person by the name of Penelope Tawney."

Elsbeth felt even more disheartened. Then again, what would it have proved anyway, if Racine had met Mum more than twelve years ago? Racine's traders were out looking for her now. It had just seemed like a clue, knowing that Mum had been so close to where she was now, rather than out there in the vast kaleidoscope, with what felt like an infinite number of Somewheres. She had felt so close to discovering more about where she might be, realising that Mum could travel too. But now it felt like the more she found out, the further away from Mum she was.

Still, it wasn't nothing. It showed that Mum could

travel. It didn't answer any of her questions about Mum, but it might be useful information. And there was the spy. She had seen Mum, Elsbeth was sure of it. *Under*, she had said. But Elsbeth didn't want to tell Racine about that yet. She didn't trust her. She was going to go and see for herself.

"It still means that Mum could travel, though," said Elsbeth. "I didn't know that before."

"You didn't?" Racine's interest seemed genuine. Elsbeth shook her head. "How very surprising," murmured Racine. But they had arrived back at the palace now. The carriage jolted to a halt.

"I have much to do," said Racine. "It is good that you were seen today, Elsbeth. The people should get to know you. I have a feeling that you will do much good for our Sphere."

Racine floated down from the carriage and Elsbeth frowned. What did she mean? Elsbeth had no intention of staying around here after Mum had been found. She hoped she would never see Racine again, if she was honest. But before she could ask what Racine meant, a servant rushed out of the front door.

"Racine!" he said. Then, seeing Elsbeth and Idris, he leaned forward and murmured something in Racine's ear.

"The Council!" exclaimed Racine. "What do they want with us?"

The servant murmured something again. Elsbeth felt a shock of fear. Had Mr Persimmon tracked her here?

Racine turned to Elsbeth. "I have some business to attend to."

"What do the Council want?" Elsbeth asked nervously.

"That is not your concern," said Racine. "We will meet for afternoon tea in the Round Room. In one hour." Elsbeth watched her disappear. Racine was fobbing her off again. One thing felt clear to her now. She couldn't rely on Racine to find Mum for her. Idris had thought that Racine could solve everything, and maybe she could, if she wanted to. But Elsbeth wasn't at all sure that Racine wanted to help her find Mum. She seemed more interested in probing what Elsbeth could do, almost as if she were testing her. There was something huge about Racine's will, she realised. It felt like a fact, like one of Mum's crossword answers. Resisting it was hard. But Elsbeth knew she had to try. She was going to have to go and look for Mum herself. And if Mr Persimmon was on to her, she had to act fast.

She went into the hallway with Idris and waited until

everyone was gone. The air was cooler here and she had an urge to press her forehead against one of the stone pillars at the side of the staircase.

Then she said to Idris, "We have to go down to the basement. I want to see what that spy meant."

"We're not allowed down there," said Idris. He shifted from foot to foot. "What if Racine sees us?"

"Are you still scared of her?" Elsbeth felt cross. Why didn't Idris understand she had to do everything she could to find Mum?

"I'm not scared of her. Well, I am a bit, but with good reason. You didn't grow up with her, remember. And this is crazy anyway. All that spy said was 'under'. That could mean anything at all! I just think you're believing what you want to believe because you want to find your mum."

"Well, wouldn't you?" Elsbeth shot back. "If you could somehow find your mums, or bring them back, wouldn't you do anything you could? This is a clue, Idris. It's *something*. Racine isn't helping me, so I have to try to find Mum myself. I can't just sit around here waiting for her. Does that make sense?"

Idris looked sombre and Elsbeth felt worried. She probably shouldn't have mentioned his parents. But she needed him to understand how she felt. He was always too scared of Racine to do anything, but she needed his help.

"You're right. I would do anything to get them back," he said softly.

"Thank you," said Elsbeth. "You don't have to come with me. But I'm going now. We only have an hour before we're meeting Racine."

Idris sighed. "Of course I'm coming with you."

Elsbeth smiled in relief. But he added, "We can't just go down the staircase where anyone can see us. This place is crawling with servants. We need to go a back way." His eyes were twinkling now. "Luckily I know one. Come on. We have to go back to the Great Library."

They moved swiftly through the palace until they were at the library again. Someone had already tidied the place up and put the books back on the shelves. Except for some bits of plaster that hadn't yet been swept up, you would never know there had been a mini earthquake there earlier.

Idris went over to one of the shelves. It was in a dark corner, behind one of the staircases. "It's around here somewhere," he muttered. He began scanning the books, tracing the titles with his finger. Elsbeth looked up at the signs above the bookshelves. They were rather different from the ones in Lewesby's public library.

Geophysical Ethics, said one label. Intelligent Plant Life, said another. She peered at the books alongside Idris. *Geology Matters: Igneous Erosion in a Post-Holocene Period.* She shuddered.

"This is it!" exclaimed Idris. He had his hand on a book titled *Weevils and Weasels: the Lost Generation*, and started to pull it out carefully.

The whole bookcase swung at an angle, revealing a dark tunnel that was sloping downhill.

"A secret passageway!" breathed Elsbeth.

"Of course," said Idris proudly. "The palace is full of them if you know where to look. Come on."

Elsbeth peered into the tunnel. "Where does it lead? Will it take us to the basement?"

Idris shook his head. "Not directly. All the tunnels are connected in a huge maze. Follow me."

They stepped into the tunnel. It was narrow, with a low ceiling, and smelled of damp earth. They had left the bookshelf ajar, and the light it cast helped to illuminate the tunnel at first. But as they twisted and turned, what little light there was disappeared, so that Elsbeth was forced to run her hands along the tunnel wall to get her bearings. The air was cool as the path led them downhill – before suddenly starting to go steeply back up. Elsbeth shook her head. "This is no good," she whispered.

"We just need to get to a crossroads," Idris replied. "Trust me, I used to escape from the dungeons often enough when I was little."

"There are dungeons down there?"

"Of course."

"Why did you need to escape from them? What were you doing in dungeons?" panted Elsbeth as they continued to go uphill.

"Racine used to put me down there to teach me a lesson if I misbehaved. I stole a skeleton key once, then I always kept it with me. That way I could at least travel to other Spheres and find food. You know, the weird thing is, I think it was a test. I think she was quite pleased when I escaped. She never used to put me back in. We'd just act like it hadn't happened."

Elsbeth shuddered. She couldn't imagine a relationship more different to the one she had with Mum. "I don't know why you're so nice, Idris."

"Well, thanks," Idris said, and Elsbeth could hear the grin in his voice.

"Look." He stopped and pointed. They had come to a crossroads, where there was just enough light to see that another tunnel wound back down the hill. "I think I recognise this one. Come on." And he bounded off,

Elsbeth close behind him.

Finally they took a turn that led them steadily downhill. The air got colder and damper. Elsbeth reached out a hand to touch the wall next to her. It was slightly muddy.

Idris stopped at a door at the end of the tunnel. "This is it," he whispered. "Be quiet. There might be a guard." Elsbeth winced as he creaked the door slowly open. It opened on to a narrow corridor with a row of doors on either side. Each had crudely cut hatches at eye level. There was no sign of a guard.

"These are the dungeons," said Idris in a low voice. "Beyond that are the meeting rooms. They have openings in them where the traders and spies come in and out."

Elsbeth looked around her. It was damp and lifeless. She shuddered. What an awful place to be locked up. Getting on the wrong side of Racine was definitely a bad idea. She had to be careful. But she also had to check the place out. Could the spy really have seen Mum down here?

They started to inch along. "We'll make our way to that doorway, then see if the coast is clear to go to the meeting rooms," whispered Idris. "But really, what are you looking for?"

"I don't know," admitted Elsbeth. "I just have to see if there is any sign of Mum. Anything at all."

"OK," said Idris. "Come on."

There was a little hatch at each closed door and, as they walked past, Elsbeth lifted each one to look inside. Each cell was the same, with a threadbare mattress on the floor and a hole in the ground that she supposed was a toilet. A tiny letter box of an air hole was at the top of each room, letting in the thinnest sliver of daylight that was barely enough to light the cell. Idris did the same on the other side. All the cells were empty, and Elsbeth felt some sense of relief at this: at least her mum wasn't imprisoned in such a horrible place.

Then Idris gasped.

Elsbeth whipped round. The shutter he had just opened snapped shut. He stood there, his face to the door, so that Elsbeth couldn't see him at first.

Then he turned round to look at her, and she knew.

She ran over, pushing Idris aside, and with trembling hands opened the shutter herself. Elsbeth stared into the dark, bare room. Bare except for one thing.

Except for one person.

There, sitting chained in the gloom, her head bowed, was her mother.

Chapter 14

"Mum!" shrieked Elsbeth. She rattled the cell door, but of course it was locked.

Mum's head shot up. "Elsbeth?" she said, staring at her wildly. "What are you doing here?" She sounded as if she were about to burst into tears. She looked exhausted. And was that a cut on her forehead?

"I've been looking for you," said Elsbeth, trying to stop herself from sobbing.

Mum stood up shakily. Her chains allowed her to just reach the door. "Elsbeth, you have to get out of here," she said. "Before Racine sees you. It's not safe for you here."

"It's OK, Mum," said Elsbeth. "Nobody knows we're here."

"Who's this?" asked Mum, looking at Idris.

"I'm Idris."

"You look so familiar," said Mum. She closed her eyes, and Elsbeth reached her hand through the hatch in the door to touch Mum's fingers. She stared at Mum, so out of place here in this prison cell on the other side of the kaleidoscope.

"Mum," Elsbeth whispered, "what are you doing here?"

Mum shook her head. "It's a long story, Elsbeth."

"I know that you were here before. With Dad," said Elsbeth. "I saw the archway, where you had your photo taken. And the kaleidoscope. Why didn't you tell me? Why didn't you tell me you could travel too?"

"I was going to tell you, of course, Elsbeth. But I hoped I would have more time. You grew up so quickly." Mum smiled through her tears. "I can't believe I didn't see the signs. I suppose I was blind to them. Part of me was hoping I would never have to think about it again. But that was wrong of me."

Elsbeth hung her head. "No, Mum. It's my fault you're even here. I was travelling to other Somewheres. I should have told you, I suppose. But I didn't think you would understand. I thought you'd be freaked out. I didn't know that people knew I was doing it. But it turned out they were watching me, and I got in trouble, and I thought they came to try to find me and took you instead."

"Oh, Elsbeth," said Mum. "None of this is your fault. I should have been honest with you a long time ago." She gave a weak laugh. "That's why I gave you the kaleidoscope. It's a tradition, in my family. It helps you to understand it, when you get the ability. But I didn't think you would start so young. And I suppose I didn't want to believe it would happen. Of course, it was inevitable – your father could travel too. But life in Lewesby was so easy, so calm. I really thought we were safe." Mum rested her head on the door.

"Who was my dad, Mum?" Elsbeth asked. "Was he not from our Somewhere either?"

"Close by," Mum said sadly. "He was from one of the HostNat Spheres near us. He was a fighter. I always meant to tell you about him, one day. I just wasn't sure how."

HostNat, where the sea levels were rising. Elsbeth wondered if her father had come from the same Somewhere as Victoria.

"Elsbeth," said Mum in a low voice, "you need to do something for me now. You need to go far away from here. Hide in another Somewhere if you have to. I'll get out and find you. But you need to stay away from Racine. She mustn't know about you. She will want to keep you here if she does."

"But, Mum!" said Elsbeth excitedly. "I can get you out of here! I have this ability to create openings. And Idris here can close them. We can get out now and go!"

But her mum shocked her. "No!" she almost shouted, before lowering her voice. "You must never do that, Elsbeth. It's one of the most dangerous things you can do."

"Why?" said Elsbeth. "Idris closed the openings I made. It was all OK."

"Those openings are powerful," said Mum. "They can cause great destruction and lasting damage to the Spheres you make them in. I know because I could do it as well. And your father could close them. But we were young and foolish. The opening we made in his Sphere set off tidal waves and people died. We swore never to do it again. You must promise me as well, Elsbeth."

Elsbeth was shocked. Her mum and dad could do what she and Idris could? So Mum had also experienced that thrill of creating the energy to make an opening. And she must have felt the fear too. She thought about never doing it again – never using this strange power she had only just discovered in herself. It felt a little like losing something. But she knew she couldn't say no to Mum.

"I-I promise, Mum," said Elsbeth.

"As far as I know, the three of us standing here are the only people in all the Spheres that have this ability," said Mum in a low voice. "It is a great power, I know, but once you use it, it rapidly gets out of control."

"But, Mum, that's not all," said Elsbeth. "Racine knows about me. She knows I can create openings."

Mum gripped the hatch. "Does she know you're my daughter?" she asked urgently.

"No! I don't think so," said Elsbeth. But as she said this, she wondered if it was true. The spy had recognised her as Mum's daughter. Wouldn't Racine have made the same connection?

Mum went suddenly still. "I hear something," she whispered. They all held their breath. The unmistakable sound of footsteps out in the corridor was getting louder. Then they stopped, right outside the doorway.

"Elsbeth," said Idris in a low voice. "We have to get out of here."

"But, Mum…"

"Elsbeth, go!" Mum said urgently.

"No, Mum! I'm not leaving without you!" hissed Elsbeth.

A key rattled in the door and a voice called, "Who's in there?"

"Come on!" Idris pulled her arm. "It's not safe. We have to hurry."

"I'll be back, Mum," said Elsbeth desperately, and she allowed Idris to pull her back to the tunnel. Elsbeth stared back at the cell door and saw Mum's fingers sticking out like a silent goodbye. Idris pushed her back into the tunnel, but the door at the other end of the corridor swung open.

A guard stood there. "Hey!" he shouted.

Idris slammed the door to the tunnel shut. Elsbeth prayed that it was too dark for him to see who they were. Racine couldn't know that they had been there.

"Run!" Idris cried.

She ran despite herself, even though every muscle in her body wanted to tear back to Mum. Mum, who she had lost and found again. But she forced herself to race along, up and up, following Idris through what felt like miles of tunnels, until they came to the hidden bookcase again. She staggered out into the bright light of the Great Library, panting for breath.

When she looked up, she found herself face to face with Racine.

Racine stood ramrod straight. Elsbeth had never

seen her look angry before – she was always calm and collected. But now she sensed a quiet fury in Racine that came out as she spoke through her teeth. "Where have you been?"

Part of Elsbeth thought she should lie, even though her shock and exhaustion were making it hard to think properly. But the truth was too overwhelming and it spilled out of her. "What is my mum doing here? Why are you holding her prisoner? Why did you lie to me?"

Racine seemed to draw herself up even taller and Elsbeth wondered if she would shout at her to get out, or attack her, or worse. Instead she said, in a strangely calm voice, "I think we should sit down. There are some things you need to know."

"I don't want to sit down," said Elsbeth wildly. "I want you to tell me what's going on. Or I'll create an opening right here, right now, and leave at once!"

Mum had said Racine would want to keep her, and Elsbeth felt that to be true. So if Racine wanted her, that meant she had value. That meant she had some bargaining power, surely. Racine didn't know that she'd promised Mum not to create any more openings.

"Very well," said Racine. She crossed the room to a table with a large leather-bound book on it and placed her hand on its cover. "This is a history of our family. We are a very old trading family, you see—"

Elsbeth cut her off. "What does this have to do with Mum?"

"You will have to listen to me, Elsbeth. You need to understand this," said Racine. To Elsbeth's surprise, she added, "Please."

Elsbeth frowned, and Racine continued.

"Traders have been in our family for generations, and the eldest sister has always taken on the role of the head of the family from her mother. I was an only child, but I had two daughters. They were both very talented. But while my youngest – Idris's mother – was docile and obedient, my eldest daughter was quite wild. Stubborn, and always getting into scrapes. Aside from her talent, Idris has always reminded me of her. Her teenage years were very difficult, and she became more and more rebellious. She told me she had no desire to be my heir, no desire to run a trading empire. She didn't care about the people here at all. She had nonsensical ideas in her head about improving other Spheres, rather than focusing on our family's mission, which is to protect and care for the people in *this* Sphere. It was on one of these do-gooder missions of hers that she met someone. Someone extremely unsuitable for her. I hated him when I first laid eyes on him," Racine declared.

Elsbeth listened to this speech with a growing sense of fear. "Who was he?" she asked softly, dreading the reply.

"Why, your father, of course," said Racine. "Larsa, your mother, is my eldest daughter."

Elsbeth took a step back. It couldn't be true. She stared at Idris and saw that he was just as shocked. "Larsa?" he said. "My aunt? I thought she had died!"

"We never had proof that she died," said Racine. "But she was dead to me. I outlawed the marriage and, when they tried to defy me, I had Elsbeth's father arrested and sent to the HostScholars."

Idris winced.

"Sent to the HostScholars?" Elsbeth asked.

"It is where people from our Sphere go for crimes against the state," said Racine. "I have to be a firm ruler, to keep the peace. It is quite an effective deterrent, as I'm sure you can imagine."

So her dad, who she had never met, had ended up in the Sphere where books were forbidden. Elsbeth thought of the spy with the eye mask and the cut down her cheek and shuddered. Had her father met the same fate – or worse?

Racine went on. "Larsa was very angry with me when she found out. She disappeared soon after, and made it seem as if she had killed herself. But I never believed it. I always kept a lookout for her. I thought she would have gone somewhere quiet. A sleepy Sphere, where she wouldn't get found."

Her Somewhere, thought Elsbeth numbly. Mum hadn't come to Lewesby from Scotland. She'd come from here. From this Sphere.

"And she was so clever," Racine went on. "For over twelve years there was no sign of her. Then the disturbances came. The ripples of travel in the kaleidoscope. They came from your Sphere, Elsbeth. We had never known of anybody with the ability to travel in that Sphere before. I sent my people, of course. I could barely believe it was Larsa. She wouldn't have been that stupid. But then we found her. I brought her back here and she confessed it all. Said that she had run out of money and had been sneaking off to other Spheres to try to find some."

But that wasn't Mum, thought Elsbeth. *That was me.* Then she realised: Mum had been trying to protect her. And instead Elsbeth had come straight here to Racine of her own accord. Straight into the lion's den.

"It wasn't until Idris here helpfully brought you to me

that I realised," said Racine. "I recognised you as my granddaughter as soon as I set eyes on you. I realised that it was never Larsa at all creating those ripples in the kaleidoscope. She had had a daughter, who I never knew existed."

Elsbeth remembered what Racine had said to Idris the first time she met her: *You finally brought something back*. She hadn't been talking about the ballerina. She had been talking about Elsbeth.

"I didn't know, Elsbeth," said Idris to her urgently. "I didn't know any of this! I swear!"

"I know," Elsbeth said slowly. She knew it wasn't Idris's fault. But this meant that Racine was really her grandmother. Her mum was really called Larsa. Penelope Tawney must have been a fake name, she realised. She felt like the dome of the Great Library was a spinning top that someone had pushed from above, making the room whirl round and round.

But in the confusion, Racine's face was clear, her eyes steely as she stared at Elsbeth. Elsbeth closed her eyes to stop the spinning feeling. She had thought she was being so careful going into the other Somewheres and taking little things for her shop. And then Idris had told her that everyone knew what she was doing. She hadn't realised that what she was really doing was putting Mum in danger. Racine's people would never have found Mum if it weren't for Elsbeth. She had been so careful to stay hidden all those years. And now she was locked up in an awful dungeon and it was all Elsbeth's fault.

"Which brings me to another matter," Racine said. "The loss of both of my daughters left me without an heir."

"What about Idris?" asked Elsbeth.

"He was without talent," said Racine. "Or at least, I thought he was, until today. But he needs you to make his ability to close openings meaningful. Without you he is nothing. And your skills at Transporting make a mockery of his. Oh, I don't mean to upset you. Idris is my blood, my kin. Though my daughter married beneath her and I fear he takes after his other mother." Racine paused. "Besides, the head of the family is passed down the female line, not the male. When I realised who you were, I thought another opportunity had presented itself. I had no heir. Or at least, I thought I did not. Until yesterday."

Racine stared straight at Elsbeth.

"Who – me?" Elsbeth said, shocked.

"But of course, my dear. You are my granddaughter."

Elsbeth shook her head and heard herself saying

"No, no, no". It wasn't possible. She closed her eyes. She couldn't believe it. What if Racine was lying about all of this?

But deep inside her she knew it had to be true. What Racine was saying fitted with what Mum had always told her. Her family was well off. They looked down on Dad. They disapproved of the marriage, then Dad had died and Mum, pregnant, had run away and sought a quiet life in Lewesby. It all made sense, except for the tiny detail that Mum was really from another Somewhere.

Elsbeth stared at Racine, so haughty and poised, still dressed in her crisp cream robes. So this was her grandmother. She couldn't have imagined a person that felt less like one. And for her to be Racine's heir? To stay here, for the rest of her life? No way. Absolutely no way.

Elsbeth stared at Racine. "I could never be like you," she whispered. "You can't keep me here." She understood now why Mum had told her to stay away from Racine. And if she knew one thing, she knew this. She wouldn't work for Racine.

Racine frowned and smiled at the same time. "You don't have to be *like me* to inherit my empire. You would simply have to carry on our family tradition.

Our family trade. My goal, Elsbeth, is for us to be the most powerful of all the Spheres. The riches we will bring to our people will be unparalleled. You could be a part of that. You see, we have enemies, Elsbeth. On either side of us. I'm sure you saw how … *dangerous* our neighbouring Spheres are. Our war with the HostScholars was a fight for freedom. They sought to make us like them. And we might have been, were it not for all the efforts I have made here."

Elsbeth remembered the chatter of the people in the streets and the happy families picnicking in the square. It was true she couldn't imagine the place ruled by HostScholars. It was full of life. She felt that Racine was confusing her.

"Every Sphere has to grapple with certain forces. You were brought up in a Sphere Between, Elsbeth, but your neighbours, as you no doubt know, face the threat of hostile technology on one side and hostile nature on the other. A Sphere can try to overcome the forces surrounding it, and succeed, but it takes effort."

Racine spoke with conviction, and Elsbeth could see she meant it. This wasn't just about Racine, or even the family. Racine believed in her empire and her people. But what about all the other Somewheres? Trading with the HostScholars, who banned books? Punishing people by sending them there to be tortured, or die, as Racine had done to Elsbeth's father? Elsbeth knew she could never be part of that.

She stared back at Racine and her eyes narrowed. "I will never be your heir," she said.

Racine paused for a moment, then said abruptly, "No. I didn't think you would agree to it. I have seen enough of your character these past two days to make me question it myself. I believe you and I are very similar. You are strong, you stand up for yourself, you are extremely talented as a Transporter. Yet you have been brought up with no knowledge – and therefore no respect – for our way of life. Your mother has clearly told you nothing about your heritage, and that is unfortunate. You are too like her – headstrong and disobedient – and I am not sure I have the appetite to break you in."

Elsbeth stared at her. She didn't think she was similar to Racine at all. And thinking of mild-mannered Mum as headstrong and disobedient didn't make sense either. But that didn't matter. Was Racine going to let her go? After all this?

"Since I saw what you and Idris could do with the openings, I have realised that there is another solution," said Racine softly. "And if you agree to it, you and your mother can go home to your little shop and live out your lives there as quietly as you like."

"What is it?" said Elsbeth quickly. She felt she would do anything – anything – to have Mum back and never see Racine again.

"My youngest daughter – Idris's mother – was my favourite. I make no apologies for that. She did as she was told, she was talented, and devoted to me and to what I was trying to achieve here. When she died, it was the darkest day of my life."

Idris was looking at the floor as Racine said this. "I'm sorry," Elsbeth found herself saying. "But what has this got to do with me?"

"One of our neighbouring Spheres is what is known as a Closed Sphere," said Racine. "The last of the BenSchol series. But while the other BenSchol Spheres are happy to make a living from sharing and trading their knowledge across the Spheres, this Sphere decided a long time ago to focus on learning and knowledge for its own sake. And so they sealed all their openings and cut off contact with the outside world."

"OK," said Elsbeth uncertainly. She still didn't see what this had to do with her. Idris was also listening with a look of confusion on his face.

"Have you ever noticed, I wonder, that there are

sometimes doubles of people in nearby Spheres? People that look just like the people from your own? Their twin, you could say."

"Oh yes!" said Elsbeth. "Like Gry's husband. I saw him here. He was very sunburnt. But I suppose that wasn't really him."

"It was and it wasn't. It was who he would have been, had he been born in this Sphere. But to all intents and purposes, yes – the same person. I have sent traders to the other BenSchol series to look for other versions of my daughter. Idris's mother. But they have traded too much with other Spheres. Their path has diverged too much from ours. They have had different unions, producing different children. But I have reason to believe that the closed BenSchol Sphere – the last of the series – will contain an exact double of my daughter. And I want to go and get her."

Chapter 15

Elsbeth's eyes widened. "You want me to create an opening – in a Closed Sphere?"

"It will not be easy," said Racine. "But I believe you can do it. And if you can, you and your mother may go. I will have no use for you any more if I can get my daughter back."

Elsbeth's face fell. She had promised Mum she would never create another opening. And to a closed world as well? She didn't even know how to do that. What if it got out of her control and Idris was unable to close it?

She shook her head. "I can't."

"Yes, you can."

Elsbeth was shocked to hear Idris's voice. He was looking at her with a flushed face. "If you do this,

Elsbeth, I can see my mums again."

"But what Mum said – you were there, Idris!" cried Elsbeth. "She said it was too dangerous – what if we killed people, like she and Dad did? I made her a promise."

"Do you remember what you said to me earlier?" said Idris. "You said that if there were some way for me to get my parents back, wouldn't I do anything I could? Well, you were right. I would do anything I could to get them back. And now I can. Please, Elsbeth," he said, his voice cracking. "Please."

Elsbeth stared at Idris, whose eyes had filled with tears. If she created this opening, he could see his parents again. She tried to imagine how she would feel if her mum had been killed, then she found out that there was another version of her in another world. To hear her voice again, to be hugged by her again. Wouldn't she do anything to see her? She knew that she would.

"Tell me the truth, Idris," she said softly. "Did you really just bring me here to show Racine what I could do? To show me off? Did you know about this Closed Sphere?"

"No," said Idris, shaking his head violently. "I promise you. I absolutely swear it. I thought Racine would help you. And, OK, I thought she would be impressed by you. I thought she'd be proud of me for finding a great trader. *I* was proud of you." His voice cracked. "But I didn't know who you were, Elsbeth. I didn't know Racine would want to keep you here. And I swear I didn't know about this Closed Sphere. But we could do it, Elsbeth," he pleaded. "We closed up the other openings so quickly, and there wasn't that much damage. Maybe your mum and dad just had bad luck."

Elsbeth shook her head in confusion. "What if I refuse?" she asked Racine, who had been silently observing the conversation between her and Idris.

"Then I shall have to train you as my heir after all," said Racine.

"I told you I would never do that."

"Then your mother will stay in that dungeon for the rest of her life. She may be my daughter, but she betrayed me a long time ago. It would be a just punishment."

Elsbeth stared up at the ceiling of the Great Library in desperation, as if it might beam down the answer to her. Refuse Racine, and she wouldn't break her promise to Mum ... but she'd have to stay here forever, or Racine would never let her mum go. Agree to Racine's deal, and she broke her promise to Mum and could threaten the lives of the people in the Closed Sphere. Maybe the best thing to do was to agree to be Racine's heir and try to break Mum out of jail, she thought numbly. Racine couldn't watch her forever. Surely there would come a time when she could make a plan to save Mum. Maybe months, maybe years into the future. But it was a horrible prospect.

Then she felt a hand on her arm. Idris stood there, a look of pleading in his eyes. "You could just do this for me," he whispered. "Forget about what Racine wants. What your mum wants. You're my only friend in the world. You've helped me so much already – you've made me feel like I was good at something for the first time in my life. You've saved my life – more than once. I know I don't have any right to ask anything more of you. But, Elsbeth – I could see my parents again. Please."

Elsbeth looked at Idris. She didn't care about what Racine wanted, and she didn't want to break her promise to Mum, but Mum didn't know about Idris, how Racine treated him, and the fact that he had nobody who cared about him. Except that now he had Elsbeth. And he wasn't just her friend, he was her cousin, Elsbeth realised. No wonder he had felt so annoying at times. He was like a younger brother.

She had always wanted a sibling and it looked like Idris was the closest she was going to get. And, right now, he needed her.

"OK," she said, though her heart felt heavy. "I'll do it."

"I'm glad you've made the right decision," said Racine crisply.

"And then you promise?" Elsbeth said. "You promise you'll let Mum and me go? For good?"

"I keep my word," said Racine. "Our family always does."

This made Elsbeth feel worse. She was breaking her word to Mum. But she knew she had to do this. For Idris, if not for her and Mum.

"Time is, however, of the essence," said Racine. "We have been contacted by a member of the Council. A Mr Norbert Persimmon. He knows all about you. And your mother. It turns out she has been a wanted woman for some years – which is no surprise to me. I have put him off – for now. But the Council are not likely to be patient for long."

Elsbeth gulped. "How will Mum escape him when you release her, though?"

Racine raised an eyebrow. "That is not my concern. You and your mother have chosen to reject my protection. You will have to find a solution yourself. I suggest you focus on the task at hand. Come," she said, crossing to the middle of the library, where Elsbeth knew an opening stood.

But Elsbeth shook her head. "I don't think that will work," she said. "If we go through an opening that already exists, I don't know how to create one inside the kaleidoscope. I think an existing opening will just lead to a dead end. I think we have to create one here and use that to get into the Closed Sphere."

Racine frowned. "My people have only just cleaned up the mess from your last opening." She sighed. "But very well. It is a price worth paying."

"Then I might as well create another opening here," said Elsbeth. "Will it take us to a Great Library in the Closed Sphere?"

Racine nodded. "It should. This palace has been in existence for five hundred years."

"OK," said Elsbeth. "Are you ready, Idris?"

He nodded and took a breath to say something, then choked on the words. Instead he smiled at Elsbeth gratefully. She smiled back. Seeing how full of hope Idris was made her feel a bit better about her decision. "Let's do this then. For your mums."

She closed her eyes and felt the energy inside her

immediately. It was always there, she realised; it was just a question of recognising it. To her surprise it seemed to shoot up out of her head much faster this time, and when she opened her eyes the shimmer stood before them and the ground was barely moving. She looked up at the sky. It was still blue. Had she learned to create openings with more control? She had been much calmer this time, rather than creating an opening when she was afraid or stressed. Maybe this wouldn't cause the destruction she had feared after all. Racine was also looking up at the sky. "I'm impressed," she said. "For the second time in a day. That is rare, I can assure you."

"Let's go then," said Elsbeth nervously. She wasn't sure how long the relative calm would last, and she was already starting to feel the ground tremble.

"Should you be coming, though, Racine?" Idris asked nervously. "Won't the Council be able to arrest you if you leave our Sphere?"

"Not if it is a new opening," Racine answered. "This will be a passageway that they are unable to monitor. It will be secure. And I need to see my daughter for myself." She glided into the opening as the other two followed her in.

Elsbeth had never been in the kaleidoscope with so

many other people before. Even being in there with Idris had felt odd. But to be so close to Racine felt uncomfortable. The air felt stuffy, as if there was only a limited amount of it.

"What's her name? Idris's mother – your daughter?" she asked.

Racine paused. "Saoirse," she said with some difficulty, and Elsbeth remembered that Idris had said that Racine had never uttered her name after she died. "Her name is Saoirse." She turned to the right and began walking round the kaleidoscope. Idris and Elsbeth followed. "Isn't it right next door if it's so similar?" wondered Elsbeth aloud.

"All the Spheres in a series are closely related," said Racine. "This Sphere is not our immediate neighbour, but because it has closed itself, I believe it to be more similar to us than the Spheres between."

Then Racine stopped and turned towards the kaleidoscope. "This is it," she said softly. Elsbeth and Idris peered at it. It looked just like any other Sphere, though it was almost all blue – the Spheres had increasingly lost the yellow mix as they went along. Elsbeth supposed that made sense, if it were the last and strongest in its series.

Racine gazed at it. "I have stood in front of this

Sphere many times from existing openings," she said. "Trying to get through to see my daughter again. I never could, of course."

So Racine had put herself at risk of being arrested by the Council, if she'd been travelling in the kaleidoscope, Elsbeth realised. All to try to see her lost daughter again.

Racine's voice had lost its ringing tone here in the kaleidoscope, where the sound was muffled. She sounded more human, thought Elsbeth. And it wasn't like her to speak so personally. But she had a chance to see her daughter again. Elsbeth couldn't imagine what that must feel like. Nor for Idris, she thought, glancing at his face. His mums had died, and now, years later, he was being given the chance to see them again.

She cleared her throat. "We should go in." She wondered what it would be like, going into a Closed Sphere through an opening she had created. "We should prepare ourselves, Idris," she said. "It might be chaotic." She tried to find a steeliness inside her, an armour that she hoped would help to control the energy of the opening as they went through. Idris nodded, looking braced, and she linked her arm through his and gave it a squeeze. "Come on," she said.

The three of them stepped into the opening. But,

as Elsbeth had suspected, it wasn't easy. She felt the Sphere resist and try to push them back into Nowhere. She gritted her teeth. She could do this. *Stay calm*, she told herself. And, sure enough, the resistance started to fall away, as if she were pushing hard at a heavy door that started to move. Then there was a sucking feeling, and with more force than usual, she and the others were pushed forward into the Closed Sphere.

◆

Elsbeth caught her breath. She had done it. Idris looked at her and squeezed her hand. They all stared around. They stood in another library. To Elsbeth's surprise everything was still. Nothing was shaking, there was no thunder above them, and the library was as quiet as any normal library at home. Elsbeth looked up and saw the kaleidoscopic pattern on the ceiling – just like the one in Racine's Great Library. This felt far more similar than the darkened HostSchol one. But it had been extended, she realised. Where Racine's library had been next to a courtyard, one wall of this library had been knocked down and opened out into a great hall.

And then there were the people. Unlike the abandoned libraries in HostSchol, where people were forbidden to enter, and Racine's Somewhere, where the books existed mostly as a store of value to be traded, this one was teeming with people in white robes sitting at desks, writing busily, or dotted around the bookshelves, putting books back and taking them out. There was a respectful silence, but Elsbeth could almost hear all the thinking going on. Everyone seemed so focused on their work that nobody had noticed the three of them materialise behind one of the staircases.

But she had dropped her concentration. Suddenly she felt the ground shake. A small but ominous rumble. "Idris," she whispered. "You should close it up quickly."

Idris, who had also been staring around in wonder, now closed his eyes and held out his hand to the opening. The rumbling increased. Some of the people raised their heads in confusion. A murmuring began. Then Elsbeth saw the shimmering opening get sucked into Idris's palm. It was closed, she saw with relief, and apparently with very little effect on the Sphere. Perhaps she and Idris were getting better at this.

But the raised heads were now turned their way, and a cry went up. "Racine!" said one of the scholars. His voice carried strongly in the silent library, echoing around the walls, and now every head in the place turned towards them. Everyone was staring at them, open-mouthed.

"Is it really you?" said one, standing up and toppling over his chair.

"How is this possible?" said another.

"An apparition! A ghost!" said a third, grabbing one of the thinner books on her table and using it to fan herself dramatically.

Elsbeth frowned. A man rushed in through the entrance of the library and stopped still. He wasn't in white robes like the others, but a dark suit, and Elsbeth wondered if he was this Sphere's version of Benedict. He cocked his head, looking at them calmly, and seemed to size up the situation immediately. Then he came up to Racine and bowed deeply. "Your Majesty," he said. "The princesses will be informed. Please, come this way."

Elsbeth and Idris followed Racine through the library to the entrance, and the scholars bowed deeply as they passed. Elsbeth looked at Idris and widened her eyes. In this Sphere, Racine was obviously an actual queen. She wondered if she would find a version of herself or Idris as a princess and prince, and suppressed a laugh. Then she remembered that the version of her mum in this closed Sphere would never have been able to leave it to find Dad. So she would never have been born. It was a relief, knowing she wouldn't bump into herself.

The Benedict version led them through a maze of corridors that felt very similar to Racine's palace. Elsbeth remembered Racine had said it was five hundred years old, so she supposed this was almost an exact replica. Then he arrived at a large wooden door. "The Long Room," he said. "The princesses are waiting."

Racine raised an eyebrow – she had remained silent throughout, which Elsbeth thought was quite a clever thing to do when she obviously wasn't sure what was going on. But now she saw that Racine was tense as well. It made sense. She might be about to see a version of a daughter that she thought she had lost forever. Idris held on to Elsbeth's arm tightly, and she felt as though he were trying not to explode with emotion.

The doors swung open and they walked into a room five times as long as it was wide, with huge windows that looked out on to the city below and seats built along the walls. Tables with reading lamps, piled high with books, were dotted around, along with luxurious cushions.

And standing in the room waiting for them was Elsbeth's mum – but not really her mum, Elsbeth corrected herself – and another woman who was clearly her sister.

"Saoirse!" breathed Racine.

"Mum!" cried Idris.

"Mother!" shouted the two women before throwing themselves on Racine and bursting into tears.

Racine looked taken aback to have these versions of her daughters hugging her so tightly. Elsbeth wondered if that had ever happened in her life. But then Racine softened and hugged them back with a fierce intensity. "It's really you," she said to Saoirse. "You are just the same."

But the version of Elsbeth's mum was equally overjoyed to see Racine. "I've missed you so much," she sobbed into Racine's shoulder. She was wearing white robes, just like the scholars in the library, and Elsbeth noticed that she was wearing what looked like exactly the same firestone necklace as Racine. After a moment's hesitation Racine embraced her as well. "You are how I always hoped you would be," she said.

It was odd, seeing her mum in front of her, but not Mum. Her hair was pulled back tightly and neatly, not like Mum's messy curls, and she moved in a different way. Elsbeth noticed that she glanced at her indifferently – which was natural, of course, as she wasn't her daughter in this Sphere, but it still felt chilling.

She wondered why the two sisters were so upset. It

seemed clear that they had not seen their real mother for some time. In fact, they were hugging Racine so intensely that Elsbeth realised that the Racine in this Sphere must have died.

Saoirse gasped, drawing back, her face wet with tears. "How is this possible?" She wasn't in white robes like her sister. Instead she wore a beautiful blue silk suit, covered with exotic birds. She really did look like a princess. "We buried you ourselves! And now you're here!"

"When did this happen?" asked Racine softly.

"Two years ago," said Larsa, who in this Sphere seemed meek and respectful. The daughter that Racine always said she wanted, thought Elsbeth.

"Mum?" said Idris. He had been hanging back, a look of hunger on his face. Saoirse looked at him, as if for the first time, and Elsbeth had a horrible feeling. It was confirmed when Saoirse said blankly, "Excuse me?"

Idris didn't exist in this Sphere. Saoirse didn't recognise him at all.

And in that instant an earthquake hit.

Chapter 16

This time there was no warning. The room was hit with a shockwave that sent everyone falling to the floor. The reading lamps fell off their tables and smashed, and Elsbeth could hear screams coming from other rooms, as if the whole palace was howling.

"Mother!" the two sisters shouted at the same time, each of them rushing to help her up. Racine looked pale – even vulnerable – for the first time since Elsbeth had met her. She and Idris pulled themselves up but another savage shake made them fall to their hands and knees.

"We need to move into the doorway!" shouted Saoirse. She and Larsa pulled Racine to the side of the wide archway at the entrance to the Long Room, and

Elsbeth and Idris crawled to the other side. They all sat huddled, facing each other.

"You must stop this!" shouted Racine to Elsbeth above the din.

"I can't!" cried Elsbeth. Idris had already closed the opening that she'd made. The slight shaking when they came into this Somewhere had obviously just been a foreshock to this, the real earthquake that creating the opening had caused. She remembered what Mum had said about the tidal wave she and Dad had set off in Dad's Somewhere that had destroyed whole towns. Had she now done the same here? How stupid she had been, thinking that she could control this!

A piece of plaster fell off the ceiling and landed next to Elsbeth with a crash. She stared at the intricate carving on it, now ruined, as more and more pieces in the Long Room plummeted down. "Cover your heads!" shouted Larsa, and they all cowered. "Please let the doorway hold," muttered Idris into his knees next to her. "Please let it hold."

And then the roof caved in.

Rubble fell around them and hit Elsbeth, cutting her hands. Dust bellowed everywhere and they all coughed, trying to breathe into their sleeves. But then, as the air began to clear, the noise of the collapse ringing in her ears, Elsbeth realised something. The ground had stopped shaking. The earthquake was over.

She looked up and saw the sky. The Long Room, or what was left of it, was on the top floor of the palace and now it was open to the elements. Its beautiful ceiling was totally gone. A chamcha – they obviously had those here as well – swooped down from above and perched on a fallen pile of books, flapping its ears a few times to fan the dust away. Elsbeth stood up, feeling wobbly.

"Careful," said Larsa. "It feels over but it might not be. There could be aftershocks."

"Thank you," Elsbeth said, looking directly at Larsa, who nodded politely. It felt so odd, looking at her mum's exact double and not being recognised at all. It almost made Elsbeth feel like she was the one who was a different person, rather than this version of Mum.

Then she turned round slowly to Idris. He had a nasty cut on his forehead but he didn't seem to have noticed. He was staring straight ahead of him at Saoirse, who was fussing over Racine. Thanks to both of her daughters, Racine seemed to have barely a hair out of place. Elsbeth and Idris were the spare parts around here, she realised. It felt very odd not being protected by someone who looked so much like her mum. She could only imagine how Idris must feel.

"Mum?" he said again. Then, when Saoirse didn't seem to hear him: "Saoirse?"

"Yes?" she said, turning to him. "You've got a rather deep cut there, I'm afraid, er…?"

The questioning way in which she asked Idris's name hurt Elsbeth. But Idris had realised what was going on. "Idris," he whispered back to her. "My name's Idris."

"What a lovely name," she smiled. "Here. Let me see what I can do." Saoirse took a handkerchief out of her pocket and began dabbing Idris's forehead with it. He closed his eyes and went still, like a cat being groomed. "I'd say you've had rather a shock, getting hit in the head like that," she said kindly as she cleaned him up. "You should be careful now – no sudden movements. If you start to feel confused, you must see a doctor. We have excellent in-house ones here. If they are all OK," she added worriedly. She withdrew from Idris, and Elsbeth saw a heavy sadness come over him.

"Do you have any children?" he asked faintly.

Saoirse beamed. "Two girls. They will take over the empire one day, as Larsa has none. Our greatest scholars devote themselves to learning, and she is one of the greatest of them all."

Elsbeth looked at Larsa curiously. She had got up

and walked to the centre of the Long Room and was looking up at the sky. Then she swung round and looked solemn.

"It seems clear what has happened here," she said. "Someone has forced an opening into our Sphere. Creating openings is known to unsettle the forces of nature, sometimes permanently. It is extremely dangerous."

Elsbeth shifted uncomfortably. This Larsa disapproved of what she'd done just as much as her real mum did.

"And the version of our mother from another Sphere has come to see us," Larsa continued. "Did we die in your Sphere, Mother, just as you did in ours?"

Racine cleared her throat, looking uncomfortable. Then: "Yes," she answered.

Elsbeth knew she didn't want to have to explain the terrible relationship she had with her real daughter to this version of Larsa.

"And why did you come here?" asked Larsa.

Racine looked slowly from Larsa to Saoirse. She opened her mouth and closed it. Then she looked at Elsbeth.

Elsbeth stared back, shocked. For what she saw in Racine's eyes was gratitude. "Elsbeth brought me here," she said calmly. "She is my granddaughter and Idris is my grandson. Together they can create and seal up openings."

"You must be very proud of them," remarked Larsa. "But do you mean that they are our children in the Sphere that you come from?" She smiled at Elsbeth. "How strange."

Tears began to fall down Idris's face. Elsbeth saw Larsa observing her, perhaps wondering why she wasn't crying too. She wondered if Larsa would realise Racine wasn't being completely truthful.

"I'm sorry," said Saoirse softly to Idris.

"It's OK," he said, his voice cracking a little. "I can tell you're not the same. I mean, you look the same and you sound the same. But you're different, you know? You don't speak the same way. I know it would be the same with my other mum too." He paused, then added with difficulty, "You're not my mum, that's the thing. My mums are dead."

Elsbeth sat down next to Idris and reached for his hand. She gave it a squeeze, and he smiled at her through his tears. "It's OK, Elsbeth," he said. "It was stupid of me really, to think it would be any different."

"It wasn't stupid at all," she said quietly.

Larsa cleared her throat. "The question is what we

do now," she said. "Was it your intention to remain here forever?"

Elsbeth looked at Racine. Was she going to tell Saoirse about her plan to take her back to her Sphere? Everything seemed different now that they had seen Saoirse in person. It seemed to Elsbeth that she would never go. Why would she? Her whole life was here.

But Racine shocked her by saying, "It is my intention to stay here, yes."

"Oh!" exclaimed Saoirse, wrapping her arms round Racine.

Larsa kneeled down and held Racine's hand to her lips.

Elsbeth looked at Racine – at her beautiful cream robe, her firestone necklace and her elegant gold rings, and realised something: she had been alone all this time. Not just alone but lonely. Here, surrounded by her children, she seemed softer – and happy. Elsbeth had never seen her look that way before.

Then Larsa turned to Elsbeth. "And you two?" she asked.

Elsbeth shook her head. "I can't stay here," she said simply. Then she looked at Idris. He held his head up. "I can't either," he said. "We have things to do." They looked at each other and smiled.

"But how will you get back?" asked Saoirse. "Does this happen every time you create an opening? It won't be safe, surely." She stared out over the rooftops at the broken buildings across the city and shuddered. "We will have to find out the extent of the damage done here. I only hope that few were injured."

With a sinking feeling Elsbeth knew that Saoirse was right. And her mum had been right as well. She thought of all the people out there whose homes had been destroyed, and maybe worse, because of Racine's decision to come to this Sphere – and her decision to help her. She couldn't control what happened when an opening was created. It could cause so much harm. How could she justify creating another one now, just to see her mum again? She had already done what Racine and Idris wanted without thinking of the consequences for so many other people and she knew she couldn't do it again. She looked at Idris and could tell he was thinking the same thing.

"At least we'll have each other if we stay here," he whispered.

Elsbeth tried to smile. But she knew what this meant. It meant that she would never see her real mum again.

But then Larsa spoke up. "There may be a way," she said slowly. "I have spent time studying the kaleidoscope and the different Spheres. Little is known about the ability to create and seal openings, as it is so rare. But it can be controlled."

"I did get better at creating them," said Elsbeth. "The first time it happened, we were in an underground prison, and I didn't know I was doing it, and the second time too, in my shop. But when we came here, I felt it happen much more quickly. There wasn't even a storm when I created the opening. I thought I had got the hang of it completely when we arrived, as there was barely a rumble before Idris closed the opening. But obviously I was wrong."

"Hmm," said Larsa. "Could the problem be not when the opening is created, but when it is closed? It sounds to me as though the disturbances are no longer happening when you create the opening – or at least, their effect is lessened. The problem may be the time it is taking to close them."

Idris's head shot up. "But that's my job," he said. He looked from Larsa to Elsbeth. "Do you mean this is all my fault? This earthquake happened because I didn't seal the opening properly?"

"Of course it's not your fault, Idris," said Elsbeth.

"What happens when you seal the opening? Can you tell us what it feels like?" asked Larsa.

Saoirse and Racine looked at Idris.

"It feels like – like I'm getting calmer. Like when I used to be upset and I would calm myself down," Idris said. He took a breath to say something else then stopped himself.

"You should tell us, Idris," said Saoirse gently. "We might be able to help you."

"Well, it sounds silly," he said. "But I used to imagine my mum singing this lullaby to me when I was little. I think of that and it makes me feel calmer."

"And you do that when you seal the opening?" asked Larsa.

"I did at first," he said. "But I try not to think about it now I have the hang of it. I feel like I should be able to do it without that."

"I don't think that's the right approach," mused Larsa. "If this memory helps you, you should keep it in the forefront of your mind as you seal the opening. If you're less distracted, the opening should seal more firmly."

Idris shrugged. "I can try."

"But should he?" asked Elsbeth nervously. "What if either of us doesn't get it right again on the way back? It's a risk, isn't it?"

Larsa inclined her head. "Is it a risk you're willing

to take? I think that's the question. Do you believe in yourself?"

Did she? Elsbeth wasn't sure. She wasn't sure who she really was sometimes. At home in Lewesby she was shy and didn't fit in with the other girls at school. But travelling to the Somewheres had made her feel more like herself. Her only real friends – Victoria, and Idris, and Mum too, she supposed, had been from other Somewheres. She had become more confident, more willing to speak up. Even more ruthless at times. She wondered whether that was because she was related to Racine. Would she grow up to be like her? Elsbeth didn't think so. She could be strong in other ways. But did she really believe she had the strength to do this?

"I believe in Elsbeth," said Idris flatly.

"Well, I believe in *you*," she said back to him. And that, she realised, was all that mattered really.

"We'll do it," she said to Larsa, who nodded solemnly.

Then Elsbeth turned to Racine. She had risen as they spoke and was sitting on a dust-covered sofa alongside Saoirse, whose hand she tightly held. "What will become of your Sphere if you stay here?" she asked Racine.

Racine looked at her. "You could still lead it. It is your birthright. Without me there you could do as you wished with it. I trust that you will keep it safe, Elsbeth?"

"I'll try," said Elsbeth. She knew she had no intention of ruling Racine's Sphere. But she could honour her promise to see that it was safe.

"I suppose I won't see you again," said Idris to Racine.

"I suppose not," she said to him. She cleared her throat. "I tried to bring you up to be proud of your heritage, Idris. I wanted you to be tough, when it seemed you were prone to weakness. It is better in life to be hard on others before they can be hard on you. I felt you needed to learn that lesson, but perhaps I was too strict. I don't know. It may have been simply that it was painful for me to look at you, because you looked so much like my beloved Saoirse."

Idris gazed at Racine as if he were seeing her for the first time and nodded slowly. "That makes sense," he said softly.

Elsbeth turned to Saoirse and Larsa. "I'm sorry about the damage," she said. The words sounded feeble – their city was half destroyed.

"We have our mother back," said Larsa simply.

"I suppose we should go then," said Elsbeth. "Are you ready, Idris?"

"As ready as I'll ever be," said Idris.

Then Racine stepped forward. "I no longer need this here," she said, unclasping her firestone necklace. She held it out to Elsbeth. "It is yours now. It is passed down from generation to generation. My people will know that you are the true ruler when they see it."

Elsbeth held the ancient stone in her hand. It was warm and seemed to throb as she clutched it. The stone was criss-crossed with a lattice of metal and covered at the top with silvery material. Elsbeth saw her own face in it, her eyes magnified.

"Put it on," said Racine, watching her.

Elsbeth knew she couldn't refuse. She hadn't promised Racine that she would take over her Sphere, but Racine seemed to think she had. She put it over her head, and the warmth of the stone rested on her chest.

It was time. Elsbeth closed her eyes, praying that she wouldn't set off any aftershocks in addition to the earthquake this Sphere had already endured. But, just like before, the energy rose swiftly and the shimmer emerged.

"Be quick," said Larsa. "And good luck."

"Goodbye, Idris," said Saoirse, smiling kindly at him.

He attempted a smile. "Goodbye," he said, but Elsbeth could tell he wanted to leave.

Then she stepped through the opening and looked

back at Racine, receding into the light and seeming at peace for perhaps the first time in her life.

◆

And then it was just the two of them. Elsbeth and Idris.

They stood together in the kaleidoscope. "Are you OK?" asked Elsbeth.

"I think so," said Idris. "That was weird, though."

To her surprise Elsbeth found herself trying not to laugh. "It really was."

Idris started to giggle too, and the two of them broke into fits of laughter as they trudged back towards Idris's Sphere.

"Here we are," he said as they turned towards the kaleidoscope, and both of them stopped laughing. Elsbeth felt nervous again. Would they cause another terrible earthquake in Idris's Sphere? Would he really be able to seal the opening more quickly this time? But she reminded herself that she believed in him. He could do it. He just needed some confidence.

"Are you ready?" she said to him. "Keep the lullaby in your mind. You can do this. I know you can."

"Thanks, Elsbeth," said Idris gratefully, and they stepped out.

They came out into an attic room in Racine's palace. The ground was shaking but Idris's hand was already outstretched and his eyes were closed. He moved with the same cat-like energy that Elsbeth had seen in him the first time they'd met, when he had swung over the banisters for the lantern. The shimmer hung for a split second longer, then swooped into Idris's palm. It was done.

Idris took a deep breath in. "Wow," he breathed. "That felt really intense."

"I can imagine," said Elsbeth. "It was the same for me."

He grinned at Elsbeth. "We're getting good at this, aren't we? Quite the team."

"Come on," said Elsbeth. "We have to go and get Mum."

Idris led the way out of the attic and down the stairs, then through the maze of corridors and rooms of Racine's palace. It felt strange knowing she was gone now and would never come back. The palace bore all her marks, but it felt empty. And also more free. Idris must have felt the same as he paused at the top of the marble staircase and then said, "No need to hide now, I suppose. We can just go down to the dungeons via the main route."

They turned round the staircase as it wound down to the lower floor. But at the bottom they were stopped by a guard. "What are you doing down here?" he snapped at Idris. "You're not allowed."

But then he saw Elsbeth and stared. Elsbeth realised he was looking at her necklace. The firestone necklace that Racine had given her. The guard stood taller. "My apologies," he murmured. "Go ahead."

They ran on, down a smaller set of stairs and through an open door that swung into the dark corridor that held the cells. Elsbeth hurried down to Mum's cell. The door was open – that was odd.

She stopped still outside it. "Mum?"

But her mum was gone.

Chapter 17

"Mum? Mum!" Elsbeth cried, stepping into the tiny cell and staring around it. There was nowhere for anyone to hide. A thought occurred to her – could there have been an opening in here? But no – she couldn't feel one, and besides, it would make no sense to put Mum in a cell with an opening. Racine would have known that. Anyway, the door had been wide open.

There was a clattering of footsteps behind them, and the guard appeared. Elsbeth swung round. "Where is my mother? Where is Larsa? The prisoner that was here."

"She – she escaped." The guard hung his head. "We did everything we could, but somebody let her out. I'm sorry."

Elsbeth was taken aback – why was he apologising to her? Then she understood – he thought she was in charge now, because she was wearing the firestone.

"Where did she go? Just tell me what happened."

"She had a visitor. And then the next time I checked she was gone. That was an hour ago. We have sounded the alarm, of course."

Elsbeth shook her head impatiently. "Who was this visitor?"

"We had no reason to suspect him, none at all," said the guard. "He had full priority access to the dungeons, so we didn't think to question him."

"But *who* was it?" Elsbeth almost shrieked.

"It was Benedict. Racine's aide."

Benedict! Idris and Elsbeth stared at each other open-mouthed. Benedict had always seemed like an extension of Racine – he seemed to exist only to carry out her every whim without asking questions. Why on earth would Benedict let her mum out of her prison cell?

"Where is he now?" asked Elsbeth desperately. Part of her was relieved that Mum was free. But where had she gone? She might have hidden anywhere, in any Sphere. She would think that she and Elsbeth were still in danger from Racine; Elsbeth had to find her to tell her that they were safe now.

"Well, here, of course," said the guard in surprise. "Naturally we arrested him." He stood back and waved his hand towards another cell behind him.

Elsbeth pushed past the guard to peer through the cell's hatch. Inside she saw Benedict standing calmly, his hands behind his back, looking as unruffled as ever.

"Well, let him out!" she said to the guard. "Go on!"

The guard stepped forward with his keys, muttering about mixed messages. The door swung open and Benedict peered out. Then he stepped forward and brushed his waistcoat down, though there didn't seem to be a speck of dirt on it. Elsbeth saw him notice the firestone round her neck, but if he was surprised he gave no indication.

"How can I help you?" he asked calmly.

"Why did you let my mum go? Did she say where she was going?"

"Your mother is a great woman. She saved my father from the HostScholars many years ago, during the war. I have always been indebted to her."

"So much so that you would betray Racine?" Elsbeth asked, curious.

The faintest flicker of a frown crossed Benedict's

face, but it was gone by the time he spoke. "Racine had no use for your mother, and she was no longer a danger to our Sphere. The only reason she was holding her in that cell was to try to scare you into working for her. But I'm afraid it became clear to me very early on that that was useless. You are going to follow your own path. I can see that."

Elsbeth wanted to hug Benedict. But she wasn't sure how he would react to that. Instead she placed her hand on his arm and said, "Thank you."

Benedict simply gave a nod of his head.

"But where did she go? How can I find her?" said Elsbeth.

"She wanted to try to find you herself but I advised strongly against it – it would only have led to her recapture," said Benedict. "So she asked me to find you – it was rather a nuisance to find myself under arrest instead – and to tell you to meet her at the shop. I believe she mentioned something about rent being due."

Elsbeth's eyes widened. The rent! After all this, Mum had remembered that the rent was due. So she had gone home after all.

"But it's not safe for her there!" she cried. "The Council are watching her – Racine said so! They could arrest her! Idris –" she swung round to him – "will you help me? We have to get back and warn her!"

"Of course I will," he said. "Come on, there's an opening at the top of the stairs."

They raced up the stairs. Elsbeth had never let the energy rise so quickly at an opening before, and within seconds they had charged into it and back into Nowhere.

"This way!" said Idris, pulling her along to the Corridor that led to Elsbeth's side of the kaleidoscope. Then they were squeezed in and pressed as before. Elsbeth made useless swimming motions with her arms to try to get through it more quickly, but the Corridor moved with its own rhythm. It finally spat them out of the other side and they moved as swiftly as they could to the familiar green and purple swirls of her own Somewhere.

"I'm not sure this is your Sphere," said Idris dubiously.

"Yes," said Elsbeth. "It is." She knew she would always recognise it now. Her home. "But where will this opening bring us out?" She remembered that the one from their shop had brought her and Idris out by the city wall, some distance from Racine's palace.

Idris shrugged. "No time to worry about that now."

He was right. They stepped forward and found

themselves on the cliffs outside Lewesby, so close to the edge that Idris nearly tottered over. "That's steep," he wheezed, looking down to the sandy beach below. Then he shivered. "And it's absolutely freezing here!"

Elsbeth squinted against the bright light glinting off the sea. It wasn't really cold, she reminded herself. It was August, after all. But having spent time in Racine's Somewhere, she wondered if she'd ever feel hot again here.

"Running will help with the cold," Elsbeth told Idris, and they set off down the narrow cliff path, leaping over rocks and dodging brambles, until they were heading, panting, up the high street, dodging tourists and locals with shopping baskets.

At Elsbeth's shop, Idris pulled her back. "Elsbeth, is this such a good idea? What if the Council arrest you too? I could go in myself and warn your mum."

"And then what? Mum and I go and hide in another Somewhere?"

Running and hiding was what her mum had done, she realised. All those years ago. Mum had suppressed her ability to travel and pretended to be someone else for so long.

But Elsbeth wasn't Mum. She was just working out who she was. She didn't want someone else controlling her life or living in fear of being caught.

She thought about Mr Persimmon. If he really wanted to arrest her, why had he been getting her to steal things for him? He had offered to help her, to keep her safe. She hadn't known who to believe back then, and when Idris had warned her that Mr Persimmon wasn't to be trusted, she had gone to Racine for help.

But she wasn't going to run away any more. She pushed open the shop door and peered into the gloom.

"Mum!" she shouted. For there was Mum, as if she'd never been anywhere else, sitting behind the counter of the shop.

She ran over and fell into her arms. Her mum's hair was wet and smelled of shampoo. She'd obviously had a shower.

Then she withdrew quickly. "Mum! It's not safe here. The Council know about you!"

"The Council?" asked Mum.

A voice came from the back of the shop. "Why is it unsafe, may I enquire?"

Elsbeth realised with horror that it was Mr Persimmon. He walked forward slowly, a strange look in his eye.

"I was just talking to this nice customer down from

Lunden," said Mum. "He's come to get some sea air. He knows an awful lot about antiques – he's in the business himself, you know."

"Mum," said Elsbeth quietly, staring at Mr Persimmon, "this isn't a customer."

"What do you mean, darling?"

"This is Norbert Persimmon. He works for the Council. He's been watching us. He wants to arrest you."

"I'm afraid your mother has been a wanted woman for some time," said Mr Persimmon. "That tidal wave she set off in HostNat had severe consequences."

Mum stared at Mr Persimmon. "It's OK, Elsbeth," she said. "He's right." To Mr Persimmon she said, "I only wanted to raise Elsbeth. I didn't want her to be an orphan. Please – take me and spare her."

Mr Persimmon's moustache twitched faintly at this, and he turned to Elsbeth. "I told you I could protect you. But you ran away."

"That was my fault," interjected Idris. "I thought you might arrest her or something."

"Hush, Idris," said Elsbeth nervously. She didn't want him to get arrested by the Council too. She was going to have to face this herself.

"It has since come to our attention," said Mr

Persimmon, "that not only have you been travelling to other Spheres and stealing things – profiting from them in your own Sphere – but you have also been creating openings. Do you have any idea how dangerous this is? The instability it causes?"

"We were closing them too," whispered Elsbeth.

"Our people have had their work cut out for them mending the rips you've created. Just as we did with your mother before you."

"Please," breathed Mum. "Please don't do anything to Elsbeth."

But Elsbeth frowned. Something didn't make sense here. "If you knew who Mum was, why didn't you arrest her straight away? And why were you getting me to steal all those things, if you worked for the Council that whole time?"

Mr Persimmon paused, then said, "We came to Lewesby because we had been informed there was a new traveller here. Naturally, when we worked out who your mother was, we assumed it was her. But I urged caution. It was I who realised that it was you, Elsbeth. I decided to see what you were capable of. You see, the Council can use people like you. And –" he turned to Idris – "like you as well."

"Me?" squeaked Idris.

"Why, yes," said Mr Persimmon. "The ability to seal up openings is as rare as the ability to create them. We have our work cut out for us, policing illegal trading activity across the Spheres. The two of you could be quite a team. You could see things you have never experienced before. Explore, travel."

"And my mum?" said Elsbeth.

Mr Persimmon inclined his head. "If she could promise us she would not engage in any illegal activity, we would agree to let her live here quietly, as she has done for twelve years."

"Of course I can promise that," said Mum. "All I want is to be here. But what is it that you expect from my daughter? You can't take her away. This is her home."

"For now she would only attend training in Lunden at the weekends," said Mr Persimmon. "And her cousin here, Idris, if he would care to."

Elsbeth turned to Idris. "Do you want to?" She knew Lewesby wasn't his home. It was too cold for him here, and he didn't know anyone. How would he feel about being so far away from everything that felt normal for him?

"Oh, yes!" Idris cried.

Mum smiled. "It sounds settled then. The children

will live here with me."

Elsbeth flew at Mum and hugged her.

Mum, seeing Idris looking at her shyly, extended an arm to him as well. "You look very much like my sister," she said. "I'm so pleased to have a nephew."

Then Mum drew back. "Elsbeth, what's this?" She had seen the firestone round Elsbeth's neck. She reached out and held it in her palm. "Did something happen to Racine?"

"Sort of," said Elsbeth. And she told Mum everything, from creating the opening to the Closed Sphere, to finding Larsa and Saoirse, the earthquake and Racine's decision to stay.

"And now there is no ruler in Racine's Sphere," she concluded. "But I did promise Racine to take care of her people." She turned to Mr Persimmon, frowning. "What will happen to everyone in Racine's Sphere? Without her to protect them?" Was it true what Racine had said? Would the HostScholars really invade if there wasn't a strong leader in place? Was Elsbeth betraying them by choosing not to go back there?

"We will send in one of our own," said Mr Persimmon. "And they will protect the Sphere. Racine told her people she was protecting them in exchange for their liberty. It doesn't have to be that way."

Elsbeth felt her stomach relax. It was all going to be OK.

Elsbeth thought of one more thing. "My father," she said in a low voice. "Racine said she sent him to the HostSchols, before I was born. There's a chance, just maybe, that he could still be alive." She heard Mum gasp.

Mr Persimmon nodded. "We can look into that. If he's there, we will find him. But you must promise me not to go yourself."

Elsbeth nodded, and Mum squeezed her hand.

"You will be hearing from me," said Mr Persimmon. He tipped his hat, then pushed the door open and was gone.

The three of them stood alone in the shop. Then Mum looked around and shivered. "Is anyone else cold?"

"Freezing," said Elsbeth.

Mum grinned. "Bet you wondered why I always used to wear scarves in the summer. I'll light a fire." Elsbeth couldn't help laughing as she went to strike the match. A fire in August.

Mum rubbed her hands together. "I've spent too long at home. It's going to take me ages to warm up again."

Elsbeth stared at her. It sounded so strange, hearing

Mum say *home* and not mean here. She was so familiar here in the shop. And yet she was that other person too. Larsa.

Elsbeth looked around. "Is everything in here real? I mean, are they all antiques from our Sphere?"

"You mean, did I ever take things from other Spheres? Like you did?"

Elsbeth nodded.

"No. It was too much of a risk. All that activity in a Sphere like this would have been bound to draw attention to me eventually. In the end it seems that you were the one to do that."

Elsbeth flinched.

"I understand why you did it, Elsbeth," Mum said. "But taking things from other Spheres is a dangerous game."

"I never wanted to be a thief," Elsbeth almost whispered, holding on to a snuff box shaped like a tortoise for support. It was true. There had been a few moments where it had seemed exciting, but she'd never been able to imagine justifying it to Mum. "And I broke my promise, Mum. I created another opening. It was terrible – there was a huge earthquake. Things were destroyed. I'm sure people were hurt."

"It was my fault," Idris spoke up. "I wanted to see

my parents again. I didn't realise that wasn't possible."

Mum stared solemnly at them both. "I understand why you did it, both of you," she said. "But you must promise me not to do it again. Or at least not without supervision."

They both nodded eagerly.

Suddenly there was banging at the door. They looked at each other in confusion. Had Mr Persimmon come back? Then Elsbeth saw black boots below the blinds of the shop door. They were unmistakably those of Mr Lennox. He'd come for the rent. The banging paused, then there was a fiddling of the lock. But Mum strode to the door before the landlord could open it. Mr Lennox stood there, looking shocked. He tried to put the key back in his pocket hurriedly.

"I hope you weren't thinking of letting yourself in, Mr Lennox," said Mum in her mildest voice. "That is not a landlord's prerogative."

Mr Lennox huffed and took a step into the shop uninvited. "I'm here about the rent. Pay up today or be served with eviction. That's my final say on the matter."

Elsbeth stared at him in anger. But Mum said calmly, "Of course." She went into the kitchen and returned with her handbag, opened it and took out a crisp wad of banknotes. Mr Lennox's eyes widened when he saw them.

Mum counted them out, and Mr Lennox shot his hand out to grab them.

"Now it's just a week until the September rent is due," Mr Lennox said, chuckling to himself before walking out.

Elsbeth swung round. "Mum! Where did you get all that money?"

Mum smiled sheepishly, dug into her handbag and opened her palm.

Elsbeth and Idris stared down at the twinkling jewels in Mum's hand.

"These are from your kaleidoscope, Elsbeth," said Mum. "I took them from my Sphere, all those years ago, as insurance. I went to try to sell them, the day that Racine's guards came and found me. I confess I had no idea how valuable they were. I only sold two for all that money, and we have dozens more. So we should put them back in."

Elsbeth pulled the kaleidoscope from her pocket. "I took it with me," she said. "It reminded me of you."

She opened it up and poured the jewels inside. She felt a surge of happiness and relief. They were safe. Mum was back and the shop was going to be OK. And

Idris would live with them now.

She caught sight of herself in the peacock mirror. She looked happy. The firestone glowed round her neck and she held it for a second. It was the first time it would be worn by someone outside Racine's Sphere, she realised. But she was going to put her powers to good use – to help everyone, not just the people in one Sphere. She was going to do things differently.

"I don't suppose they have cardamom rolls in this Sphere, do they?" asked Idris. "I'm starving."

Elsbeth's mum laughed. "No. But I'm fairly sure I can remember the recipe. I'll help you bake them. Come on, Elsbeth." And they went into the kitchen, leaving the kaleidoscope on the counter, its light casting flickers of rainbows around the shop.

Acknowledgements

I would like to thank my writing group in Washington DC, Jeanne Hargett and Laska Hurley, where the first draft of this book was written, for their encouragement and enthusiasm throughout.

Thank you to my London writing group, Becca Langton and Julia Tuffs, for emergency brainstorming, emergency drinks, and emergency industry gossip sessions.

A special thanks to younger readers Anna Hargett and Ava Viding-Rogers for their time and feedback in reading early drafts.

Thank you to Laura West for seeing potential in the kaleidoscope, and thank you to my superstar agent Zoe Plant for all her tireless work on my behalf.

Thank you to Tom Bonnick, whose email made me cry in Rome when I realised this book would be published, and thank you to Fiona Scoble for her careful edits and to the whole team at Nosy Crow.

And finally thank you to both my children, Greta and Ranald, for being pretty decent nappers when I was writing and redrafting while they were babies: if you hadn't slept, this book might never have been.